Virginius Dabney

Gold that did not glitter

A Novel

Virginius Dabney

Gold that did not glitter
A Novel

ISBN/EAN: 9783743322301

Manufactured in Europe, USA, Canada, Australia, Japa

Cover: Foto ©Andreas Hilbeck / pixelio.de

Manufactured and distributed by brebook publishing software
(www.brebook.com)

Virginius Dabney

Gold that did not glitter

GOLD

THAT DID NOT GLITTER.

A NOVEL.

BY

VIRGINIUS DABNEY,

AUTHOR OF "DON MIFF."

PHILADELPHIA:

J. B. LIPPINCOTT COMPANY.

1889.

GOLD THAT DID NOT GLITTER.

I.

He was One of the Finest.

And whenever he swung jauntily along his beat, carelessly twirling his persuasive locust, house-maids ceased, for a moment, polishing window-panes, baby-carriages stood still, cooks peered through basement windows. For the brass buttons stood high on his bold chest, and the blue cloth lay flat and smooth on his broad back. Trim was his moustache, too, elastic his tread, and the roses on his cheeks made a pretty contrast with the azure of his laughing eyes.

But, although he was considerably under thirty years of age, Delany's figure had already begun to hint that he was not to escape the fate of policemen; for already had grace of outline begun to give way to solidity of form. So he puffed a little as he mounted the flight of steps that lead from the river level to the terrace which overlooks East River at the foot of Fifty-First Street. When he reached the topmost step, or, rather, the one next the last, he gave a good strong puff, and, leaning on the parapet, cast his eye carelessly up the street.

Night had fallen, though somewhat prematurely; for black clouds veiled the sky, from which was floating down, flake by flake, the first snow of the season.

There were not many people on the street, —here a man stalking home to his dinner, there a woman scuttling along to save her new winter bonnet. Blocks away a lamplighter hurried from post to post. In the nearer distance a messenger boy sauntered, whistling.

All these the professional eye of the officer took in at a glance, lingering, however, upon one figure,—that of a young man who approached with bent head, and staggering from side to side.

Definitions are proverbially difficult. A hundred philologians will give you a hundred equivalents of the simple word drunk, for example; their wives a hundred more. For the definition of this word, as of others of an objurgatory tendency, is apt to be a sort of etymological lasso, of which you hold one end while the other nooses your friend.

But a policeman is not a philologian. A man of action, rather; and, as such, he has adopted, in reference to what constitutes drunkenness, a very simple working hypothesis: if a man falls half a dozen times in one block and rises after each tumble, whose business is it? Men, meeting him, may smile, women shrink, affrighted, against the wall, troops of boys follow in his zigzag wake, jeering joyously; but the guardian of the peace sees him not. But let him fall once too often,—fall and rise not,—and he straightway becomes a professional fact.

So Delany, rested now, takes the last step of the stone stairway, and goes sauntering up the street, carelessly twitching the leathern thong of his club, with head thrown back and eyes fixed on the lowering clouds above.

About forty or fifty feet from the terrace is a lamp. Under this the two men met; and although Delany, with his eyes riveted upon the clouds, swerved considerably to the right, a sudden lurch of his *vis-à-vis* brought their shoulders together. Even so, the stalwart officer, with a momentary glance to the left, was passing on without a word.

"I beg your pardon," said the young man, quickly; and then, raising his eyes and seeing that a policeman stood before him, he staggered back with a troubled look.

A flash of interrogation swept across the roundsman's intelligent face as he heard the words and saw the look.

The two men bowed and passed on.

But Delany had lost his interest in the sky. With head bent forward and pursed brows, he moved slowly forward. Presently he stopped, and, half turning in his tracks, looked back over his shoulder. The young man was doing the same thing, and their eyes met. Each quickly turned and moved forward again.

But something was on the policeman's mind; for he had not gone forward five paces before he stopped again, and stood still, meditatively tapping the snow-clad pavement with his club. Suddenly he wheeled about and fixed his eyes upon the retreating figure. He watched it for a moment, then moved forward two or three steps, then halted again, then a few more steps in advance; till, presently, coming to a decision apparently, he threw back his head and began to follow, with slow and measured stride.

"Shure, and you won't be after runnin' the poor mon in? Lave him in pace! a drop or so too much, yis; but what o' that?"

"And is it you, Maggie darlin', as would be interferin' with a member of the force in the discharge of his duty?" And Delany, diverted from his half-formed purpose, whatever it might have been, sauntered leisurely across the street to where a rosy-cheeked house-maid stood in an area, her arms resting on the railing.

"He is a bit full, that's a fact, cap'n," said Maggie, with her eyes in the direction of the terrace.

"And it's full he was, think ye? But full and impty, impty and full, they come much to the same sometimes, Maggie mavourneen."

"Shure, and you don't mane to say the gintleman was starving; for he was a gintleman, intoirely, by the cut of him?"

" And it's meself as would be proud to starve foriver for that swate and tinder look, Maggie !"

" Be done with your flatthery, mon, and tell me how ye know 'twas imptiness ailed him ?"

" And wasn't it meself that saw his face under the lamp ?"

" And the lamplighter is just lightin' it now !"

" The lamplighter, is it ? And what nade of the spalpeen, with Maggie's eyes across the way ?"

" Och, the blarney of the mon !" laughed the delighted Maggie.

" Blarney is it ?"

" Yis, and the same to every gurrl on your bate !"

" Divil a bit, divil a bit of it, Maggie darlin' !"

" And what were you a-sayin' to the cook, thin, on the next block, as you came down a bit ago ? Oh, the desatefulness of a mon !"

"Desavin' the widow Flaherty, was I? And all I tould her-was that I thought we were goin' to have some weather! And wasn't it snowin' at the toime? Desatefulness, indade! Och, but the cruelty of a woman! But run in, Rose of Killarney, or ye'll be catchin' a heavy could in that white throat; shure, and the very snow blushes for shame when it lights on it! and thin milts with tinderness,—small blame to it!"

"Off with ye, flattherer!" but she added, as he moved away, "The desaver! But it's a swate tongue he has in his head, has Delany!"

II.

In a great cosmopolitan city a mere par-
tition-wall ofttimes curtains apart most diverse
fates. Here an infant utters shrill protest
against a world it knew not an hour ago;
while, next door, and not three feet away,
an octogenarian breathes his last weary sigh.
In this dainty chamber, the cooings of a
honeymoon; in that, the ragings of jealousy.
And Joy heareth not the cry of Anguish,
nor Anguish hers.

And while Maggie sat at the basement
window, smiling still, and wondering whether
the approaching postman would be able to
match the sweet cajoleries of the roundsman,
a scene far different from the one we have
just witnessed was enacting down by the
river's brink. Close to the water's edge
stood the young man whom we have just

seen staggering along the street. The dark waves are surging at his feet. His hands are clasped and his upturned eyes are drinking in, from the black firmament above, a despair that is blacker still. Let the impassioned words that his trembling lips sob forth go unrecorded.

And now he is done. He has muttered his last prayer. With a frantic gesture he covers his eyes with both hands, as if to shut out the view of the pitiless river in front. And then, throwing up his hands with a low wail, he lowered his head for the irremediable plunge; and in an instant he was whirled three feet from the water's edge by a powerful arm that girdled his waist.

In New York the laws provide no penalty for suicide; but a clumsy attempt at it is a felony. This the young man knew.

"You can't do that!" said a voice at the back of his neck.

"Can't do what?"

"Why, drown yourself!"

"Who told you I wished to drown myself?"

"Who told me? Haven't I eyes?"

"Eyes or no eyes, I defy you to prove it!"

The young man had been struck by the quick, inquiring glance of the policeman, and by his turning for a second look. Naturally, therefore, his first thought was that he had followed him; but how had he managed to creep up behind him unobserved? He was nabbed; that was clear. But why had the officer removed his coat? For the stout arm that held him was clad in a shirt-sleeve merely,—a sleeve ending in a snowy, polished cuff looped with costly buttons. And— stranger still—no boot covered the stockinged foot planted so firmly by his own! and the snow was falling heavily!

"Who are you?" asked the young man, trying to twist himself into a sight of his captor's face.

2

"A friend," replied he, slightly relaxing his grasp. And the two men, with legs interlaced and bodies touching, leaned back for a look, each at the face of the other.

There was a vivid contrast between the two: on the one side, pallor and that strange glitter in the eyes that emaciation gives; on the other, perfect health and vigor. For a while neither· spoke. Presently the pale young man said to the other,—

"What were you doing here, in this garb?"

The captor started. He was silent for a moment, then raised his eyes to those of his prisoner; then, slowly,—

"In the excitement of seizing you, I had forgotton why I was here. But, as I have surprised your secret, perhaps honor requires that you should have mine. Can you believe me when I tell you," continued he, with a sad smile, "that my errand was the same as yours?"

The young man gave a cry of amazement: "*You!*" and with a quick glance he took in the handsomely-dressed figure before him.

"Yes; and but for a policeman who loitered about the foot of those steps for some time, it would have been all over with me before you came. When he disappeared behind the terrace, I took off my coat and shoes, and was about to plunge in, when you appeared, I then scrambled into that depression, hollowed out in the stones by the waves, and lay crouched there till you should pass on. When I saw that you, too——"

"But why on earth——"

"Ah, that I cannot tell! Mere instinct, I suppose. But not altogether. Lying within a few feet of you, I could not but overhear your farewell words; and those words convinced me—pardon me—that you were about to commit a crime. A man who has a mother and sister to pray for, has no right to die by his own hand."

"You are right! I thank you!"

The two men, with warmly-clasped hands, stood silent for a while.

"But," resumed the last speaker, "my motives were not altogether bad. I had a mother and sister to support, but could get no work to do, and *they* were supporting *me!* —and at the cost of the cruellest privations. But I should have endured to the end; yes, I admit that. Something might have turned up. But my head had grown so dizzy through want of food——"

"Want of food?"

"Yes; for three days not a morsel has——"

"Merciful God! Here, come along with me!" cried he, seizing his arm. "Wait a moment: I forgot my shoes and coat. Here they are,—all right! Now come on." And, grasping his arm, he led the young man towards the steps. As they ascended, he put his arm round his waist; but even this support was insufficient, for, when they reached the first landing, the young man's limbs gave way, and he sank down, with a sigh, upon the stone steps.

"Let me rest a moment," said he, in a tremulous whisper; and, covering his face with his hands, with his head resting in the snow, he sobbed silently. His companion, waiting for the shock of reaction to pass, sat down beside him, without a word. But there was yearning in his eyes; and presently he laid his soft, white hand upon his head.

The prostrate figure thrilled.

Just then a shadow fell upon them from above; and, looking up, the rescuer saw a policeman leaning over the parapet. Rising quickly, and hurrying up to the officer, the two men conversed in undertones for a moment, then descended the steps. A few minutes later and the three men were moving slowly up the street, the sufferer supported, in part, by the other two. A basement window flew up.

"Shure and you are not goin' to run the poor man in, captain, afther all?"

"Yis; and it is here that I am afther runnin' him in. Have ye a little soup, Maggie? Yis? Then open the door quick; for its starved intoirly is the young gintleman."

A rapid fluttering of skirts was heard, and in a trice the grilled basement door flew open. The three men entered the front room, and our young friend dropped heavily into a chair. Maggie and her sister (the cook) flew from sitting-room to kitchen, back and forth, like wild birds in a cage. Never was table more quickly served. When the young man saw the steam rising from the hot soup, his eyes glistened, his lips twitched; and when the officer took him by the arm, he rose and staggered eagerly towards the table. Seizing the spoon, he began to devour the soup with a haste that would have been unseemly had it not been pathetic; and his hand trembled so that little of each spoonful reached his lips. His face wore the fierce look of a wild beast feeding.

Nothing lends such elegance to our manners at dinner as a hearty luncheon.

The soup was splashing everywhere. Maggie, with deft fingers, pinned a napkin over the young man's breast.

It might have been this act of thoughtfulness, or else the overwhelming effect of the food; but the young man bowed his head and averted his face, while his clinched fists, pressing heavily upon the table, shook violently. A rain of silent tears poured down his cheeks. The four spectators turned away, the two women with their aprons to their eyes.

Presently the rapid click of the spoon began again. The policeman lightly touched one of the broad shoulders of the man who stood looking out of the window:

" I'll be afther hailin' the cab for ye now ?"

" Thanks, very much," said the English-

man; for such he obviously was, notwithstanding his dark hair and eyes.

In a few minutes the sound of rattling
wheels suddenly ceased in front of the house.
The young man was just finishing his second
supply of soup, and, as he scraped the
bottom of the plate, cast, between spoonfuls,
wistful glances at the cook; but the Englishman checked her with a motion of his hand.

Hearty thanks and godspeeds over, the
three men were passing through the door.

"A worrd with ye, captain," said Agnes,
the cook, laying two fingers upon the officer's sleeve: "what say ye to a wee drop
o' the craythur for the young gintleman?
Me mother gave us a little jug when we
left the ould country, and it's there in the
cupboard."

"Poteen? County Galway? Bless the
darlin' soul of ye, it wouldn't harrm the gintleman,—no, nor a baby. Poteen is it?
Bless the swate name of it, it wouldn't hurrt

even an innocint polaceman—of a snowy
noight loike this!" and he filliped a flake
from his sleeve.

"Och, the awful chake of the mon!"
laughed the two girls, with genuine Irish
delight in mother-wit.

A queer little jug and three glasses were
now produced. But the jovial Delany insisted that the two girls should do honor to
the ould country,—just a wee drop, gurrls,—
and two more tumblers were brought forth.

"And here's to County Galway,—and it's
sorry I am for the b'ys ye lift behind ye; it's
wapin' and cryin' they are, poor lads!"

The Englishman lingered behind when the
officer and the young man passed through
the door.

"You will be sending something soon to
cheer your old mother's Christmas; please
add this from me," said he, thrusting a folded
bank-note into the hand of each of the girls.

"Oh, surr, we can't accept anything——"

"Certainly not,—send it to your mother;" and he closed the door behind him.

The two girls, in spite of the snow, went out into the area to see the party off.

"Which way, boss?" asked the driver.

"Café Moretti."

"Café Moretti?"

"Yes,—on Fourteenth Street, opposite Tammany Hall!"

"I'm bound ye know where that is," said the policeman; "loikely ye are a cousin o' the boss!"

Cabby winked, and the girls laughed.

"And mind you, lively, lively," said the Englishman, dropping half a dollar into cabby's palm and springing into the hansom. The driver telegraphed the good news to his horse, and he turned the corner almost at a gallop.

The girls unfolded their notes, and started with pleasure when they read the figures.

III.

THE rapid jolting of the hansom, the hot soup, the (not so very) wee "drop o' the craythur," drove despair from the heart of the young man, and hope flowed in in a mighty tide. Turning to the man who had saved him from what he now shuddered at as a frightful crime, a grateful mist dimmed his eyes.

"How *can* I ever thank you sufficiently!"

His companion turned upon him a grave, kind smile: "You feel better?"

"Better! words cannot express the change. Every cloud seems to have rolled away. Those people passing along the street no longer appear to me as enemies. I feel it in my bones that I have not been saved in vain. Something is going to turn up, as Mr. Micawber would say."

The Englishman laid his hand upon the other's knee. "Something *has* turned up. It so happens," continued he, observing the puzzled look of his companion, "that I have enough of this world's goods to keep us both going for some little time. A perfect stranger, no claim, you say? Hardly that; for, while I was rescuing you, you were saving *my* very valuable life."

"I hope I *have* saved it—for good?"

"That depends on you."

"On me?"

"Yes. If your life turn out to have been worth saving, I shall deem mine worth living. I see you don't understand. Perhaps I may explain after we have dined. By the way, how is your appetite?"

"I had lost the feeling of hunger, but that soup has made me as ravenous as a wild beast. I believe that if I were gnawing a bone," added he, with a rather ghastly smile, "and you looked at me, I should growl!"

"We'll soon stop your growling."

"How far have we to go? Ugh!"

"Here we are!"

IV.

THE Café Moretti occupies the second and third stories of a building originally a dwelling-house.

"The approaches are not imposing," remarked the Englishman, as they reached the first landing and came in full view of the scullery (once a bath-room), and, beyond that, saw the busy cooks hanging over the wide range, from which savors rich and rare floated down the hall-way; "but never mind; 'the proof of the pudding,' you know!"

When the two friends entered the dining-saloon, they found every table occupied. A waiter suggested the room up-stairs; but Tenterden (the Englishman), seeing Signor Moretti in the kitchen, went there to consult him. While he is absent, let us take a glance at things. As for our fasting young friend,

26

he has eyes only for the tempting dishes
that he sees before him.

In the ornamentation of the room chance
has reigned supreme; and the result is such
as would make an æsthetic decorator rage.
The mantel-piece in front of you is loaded
with heterogeneous objects, among which a
hasty glance detects, to the left, a carved
white elephant tranquilly waving welcome
with his wrinkled trunk; while to the right,
a big, tawny, terra-cotta owl fixes upon each
new-comer a look of ferocious and eternal
surprise. For when, amid all the feasting, is
his turn to come? Where are the rats and
mice and such small deer?

And if you would forget you are in
America, lift your eyes and meet those of
tempestuous Salvini, who glares down upon
you from the wall in front. Near him hang
peacefully, side by side, Cavour and Mazzini,
—and rightly, too, for both loved Italy the
Beautiful; and not far away, the shaggy,

grizzled beard and little red cap of Garibaldi.
Near this trio a photograph shows you the
features of the presiding genius of the place;
while a couple of prints in the corner set
forth the comic troubles of a cook. See,
too, near the ceiling, the bland face of the
incomparable Mario; lower down, the form
of stalwart Campanini; and, far away in the
corner to the left, two counterfeit present-
ments of Patti the Divine; one as a girl of
sixteen, when, as a rising star, she twinkled
just above the horizon; the other showing
her gazing serenely from a window, world-
renowned and more or less married.

And what a contrast on the other side of
the room! There two rival railways spread,
side by side, their alluring maps! Who
hung them there? Was it the Young Men's
Christian Association? Would they remind
us that all of us must some day bid farewell
to New York—and to Moretti?*

* Since this passage was written Signor Moretti has

But the contrasts among the guests are quite as strange. Let us have a look at them. You will not see the same people here to-morrow night. One cannot manage such a dinner two days in succession. So, at a theatre; the seats are occupied every evening, but the faces change.

Let us study that group of six at the table by the window,—a middle-aged couple, two stalwart young men, and a pair of lovely girls. The married couple have been here before. It is equally obvious that the two merry maidens are making their first incursion into this fascinating land of Bohemia. Their faces are flushed with pleasure, their eyes sparkle with a mixture of curiosity and amusement, as they watch the various groups of diners.

"Oh, look!" Their forks fall, jingling, upon their plates. Their soft hands are

---

given up the rooms I have described, and taken others, —where I shall not tell; for whoso deserves one of his dinners will have the genius to discover him.

clasped in breathless delight; for the ador-
able tenor who has made their hearts go pit-
a-pat in Lohengrin stalks into the room,
with a pert little dog at his heels. But, oh,
horrors! Does *he* eat? No; he has merely
lounged in; and, with a wave of his hand to
the waiter, takes his stand by a dark-eyed
party of three in the corner next the kitchen,
—two gentlemen and a lady. A waiter will
tell you who they are,—a basso, a stage
manager, and an illustrious daughter of
Terpsichore,—she whose twinkling, fantastic
toe has so often caused to drop, in rapt admiration, the under-jaws of the bald-headed
widowers who crowd the front rows of the
orchestra stalls.

Oh, they are having a tremendous lark,
our two laughing beauties! How much they
will have to tell when they get back to New
Haven; for all the way from there have they
come, with two Yale men to do the agree-
able, and their uncle and aunt to play pro-

priety. It is no novelty to the jolly New York couple. They have neither chick nor child, and have grown gray poking about in all sorts of odd corners in quest of the dainty and the toothsome. No small Æneas plays before them in their halls; but they can at least eat.

The wind is tempered to the shorn lamb!

Behold, too, those Statesmen assuaging their toil over a *fiasco* of unaccustomed Chianti. Their thick necks, their short noses, their long upper lips, reveal them as members of our dominant race. And who can blame them for being such? Have they ever, in the long ages, ruled anybody, even themselves? Give them a chance! Let them try their hand; while we natives, freed from the fatigues of self-government (a whole weary, weary century of it!) pursue, with single-hearted zeal, the nimble, the fugacious, the divine dollar!

A mixed company, one would say. Yes;

but one in this; all are glad to be there, all glad to see you come; for does not every eye greet you as you enter, and say, Ah, here's another who knows what's what?

But here comes Tenterden, and with him Moretti, with a napkin under his arm; nodding, with a smile, to right, to left. He is rejoiced to see them all; even that barytone, who lost his voice six months ago; and that ballerina whose sprained ankle prevents her from earning a living. "Are they the less hungry for that?" asks Stefano Moretti. "Ha! Let them eat!"

Yes, they could have the little room, all to themselves. A party of four had engaged it, but had sent a telegram to say they could not come.

Four covers had been laid, but there was hardly room on the little table for the plates, so generous was the supply of *hors d'œuvres* that cover it. Plump olives, dishes of Bologna sausage, of anchovies fresh from their bath of olive oil, bunches of celery, crisp and snowy, radishes, firm, brittle, and cold, and I know not what besides. Bread, of course, and butter, and, in the middle of the table, a bouquet in honor of the party which had been expected.

"These things are to whet your appetite," remarked Tenterden.

The sharp click of a fork was the only response.

Soup next, and, after soup, fish,* and then —shall we burst into song, O muse?

"What is this?" asked our young friend, breaking his eloquent silence.

And with the stem of his goblet he was pointing towards an engraving of Venice, bride of the sea, while his grateful eyes rested upon Milano, *patria* of Moretti; and the dark flood of the rich wine of Chianti pours along his parched throat. Not other-

---

* Comes later,—but no matter.

c

wise sweeps a thunder-shower adown a dusty cañon.

"Spaghetti."

"Spaghetti? How am I to eat it?"

"Any way you can." And Tenderden, resting his cheek upon his hand, watched the efforts of his *vis-à-vis* with a smile. "Ah, that's right!" he added, as the rear ends of a long mouthful disappeared, almost with the click of a whip.

The young man laid down his fork and looked at Tenterden.

"How do you like it?" asked the latter.

"By Jove!" and he finished his answer with his fork.

Presently he was helping himself to a fresh supply; but Tenterden quickly removed the dish out of his reach, and, calling a waiter, handed it to him: "Open the champagne, please."

The young man's eyes sparkled with

pleasure as he looked upon the goblet of liquid amber bubbling before him.

"May I take the liberty," said Tenterden, "of proposing the health of your mother and sister?"

"Ah, thank you," replied the young man, with effusion (they had already made away with a quart of Chianti); "I wish you knew them." And he lifted his glass. Then, coughing,—for the champagne-gas choked him,—"I think—you would—like—them."

"I am quite sure of that," said Tenterden, bowing. "Ah, here come the *entrées!*"

By ordinary mortals *entrées* are served one at a time. But Signor Moretti is a law unto himself, as well as unto those who love him. Like the king, he can do no wrong in their eyes. And he sends you in three at once.

It is not worth while to discuss the matter. As well condemn the grave-diggers' scene in Hamlet to a Shakespeare scholar; for, to his disciples, Moretti is the Bard of Avon, the Beethoven, the Michael Angelo of mine hosts.

Three bountiful dishes at once!

And, as they are placed in front of you, there rise, before the wondering and entranced nostril ineffable harmonies—vague—ravishing—Heliogabalic!

"Umgh!" cried Willis,—an impromptu grace, let us hope.

"These," explained Tenterden, "are Milano cutlets; that, fricasseed chicken, with mushrooms; these, kidneys,—*rognons sautés.* Which will you begin on? Ah, here comes the signor himself!"

Moretti had stopped to speak to two gentlemen in the main room.

Of these, one was slender and of dark complexion, with close-cut black hair and beard, who wore glasses over eyes that did not seem to need them,—the clear, steady, all-seeing eyes of an artist, if one might guess at his profession.

That's half the fun of dining at Moretti's, —guessing who and what people are.

For everybody, there, is somebody. Fools never go—or go but once.

" *Then how does he make a living ?*"

I have not time to go on the stand; let us move forward with our story, rather.

The artist's companion is his antithesis. Jocund, rubicund, and rolypoly,—as he sits there, he smiles,—not with his eyes alone, but with smooth, full knee, with haughty waistcoat, as well. Even across his broad back you shall see Merriment time and again go dimpling!

A retired banker, without a doubt! No sordid cares throttle *his* heart! Let us rejoice with him, brother men, and not go envying the gods!

A moment before, a waiter had brought, as a special compliment to this serenely joyous plutocrat (but *not* because he was rich), an extra dish.

"Aha! chicken livers *sautés!*" ejaculated the artist; and, raising his eyes to his friend's face, and filling his glass with champagne (for he, not the financier, seemed to be standing treat), he watched, with a half-twinkle in his kindly eye, the look of dim, religious awe that shaded his companion's visage, when he pressed, between palate and tongue, a savory lobe.

"*Ah, come sta, maestro?*" cries Moretti, laying two plump fingers on the comfortable shoulder of the millionaire.

"*Grazie, signor, sta bene. E voi?*"

Oho, an Italian!

Perhaps. But one swallow does not make a dinner, as, likely enough, the Chinese put it.

"The maestro thinks they are not bad," remarks the artist, pointing to the dish.

"Ha!" abstemiously chuckled the *cordon bleu,*—who, so lavish with his three *entrées* at a course, paradoxically allows himself but one *ha* to a laugh.

But that one covers the ground,—meaning all things,—annotated by the accompanying smile, that tipped you a wink from every dimple.

"Come in, signor," called Tenterden, "and join us in a glass of champagne; this is my friend, Mr. Willis, of Virginia."

"Oh, Richmond! Ha! you know Zetelle?" [Richmond's Delmonico.]

"Zetelle! Do you know him?"

"Oh, yes,—from Milano, like me."

"But Zetelle is a Greek——"

"Does he say that? Ha!"

There is a kind of freemasonry among the diners at Moretti's. Whatever your neighbor may be, he is not an ass or a sham,—and to know that is half a letter of introduction. So, when the *chef* passed down the room, benignly smiling, greeting new-comers with a bright glance, nodding to this group or to that,—exhaling good nature from every pore; and when one of our friends, filling his glass, said "Let us drink his health;" it did not seem strange that the two gentlemen at the other table filled theirs also, with a "Yes, may he live forever." And, amid applause, four glasses went up, and smiles beamed from table to table, and friendly nods were nodded; in the midst of which the maestro tried to quote this passage of Cicero on Roscius: *Propter excellentem artem videbatur omnino mori non debuisse,*—but (owing to enthusiasm) could not quite recall the words.

And after the ruffed grouse, came Roquefort cheese and oranges; then coffee; and, with the coffee,—

"I am sorry for people who do not smoke," quoth Tenterden.

"I can't believe," said Willis, dropping back into his chair, with a contented smile, "that I was ever hungry in my life."

V.

"THAT reminds me; as we were driving down in the cab, I begged you not to tell me your story till after we had dined. It is trying both to tell and to hear sad things on an empty stomach. Now we are ready for the fray," continued he, smiling; "but, before you begin, I will say one word——"

One word isn't very much (always excepting the Aristophanic for hash), but Tenterden seemed to have some difficulty in finding the one he sought. After shifting his cigar from the east to the west corner of his mouth once or twice, however, he snatched it suddenly from under his dark moustache, and rather blurted out,—

"Of course I know that you are deucedly hard up, and all that." Then, resting his head upon his hand, he was silent for a little while. Presently, sitting bolt upright, and his face cleared of the wrinkles of perplexity, he said, in a quick, business-like way,—

"Well, we will settle *that* matter, now. Do you owe any little debts?"

"I owe my landlady two weeks' board. But," added Willis, a little eagerly, "the contents of my trunk would have saved her from loss."

Tenterden gave him a quick look, rose, pulling at his moustache, made a turn or two in the corner of the room, snapped his lowered head up and down with something that had the sound of muttered oaths; then, wheeling suddenly upon Willis, with a fierce look, as though he blamed *him* for it:

"This is a marvellous good world, Mr. Willis! How proud I should be if I had made it!" And, seizing a match, he relit his cigar with savage puffs.

"Two weeks' board?" resumed he, sitting down. "Anything more?"

"That is all—that is to say—yes, two weeks' board."

"'That is to say?' Go on. I must know all."

A deep flush overspread Willis's face.

"Go on!"

"My overcoat is in pawn."

"And this is December!"

Tenterden shut his eyes, twisted his head aside, and seemed to be swearing, inaudibly, at something or somebody.

"Your overcoat. Anything else?"

The color flashed out of Willis's face: "Yes, a gold watch,—old and not very valuable, I dare say,—only——"

"Only?"

"The fact is, it was—my—father's watch," said Willis, pale and with downcast eyes. "That is all."

"And the 'demned total' of all your indebtedness?"

Willis added up the items.

"Fifty-seven dollars," repeated Tenterden. "Well, I shall lend you that amount." And, going down into his pockets, he drew out a wallet and began to count out the notes. "There, I lend you an even hundred,—easier to remember, you know. I have just one hundred left in my purse. By the way, you may wonder why I carried such a sum with me — under — the circumstances. Vanity! nothing but vanity! I shrank from the announcements in the papers: 'A toothpick and eleven cents in cash was all that was found in the pockets of the deceased.' All of us worship money; even I, you see, who profess to despise it. By the way, it would be putting it rather big to say that I am lending you a hundred dollars. You might claim to be making me a present of one hundred, since but for you, the entire two hundred——"

"I assure you that even to accept as a loan——"

"Stop," said Tenterden, holding up his hand. "The very expression of your countenance convinces me that you are on the eve of saying something silly. You must know," added he, tapping his forehead, " I am a mind-reader; and I can distinctly see the most absurd words bubbling up from your brain! Certainly,—no objection to shaking hands if you wish it——"

" *Buona sera*, Signor Moretti!"

" *Ah, buona sera, maestro,—a rividerla! Ha!*"

The rosy-nosy maestro was shaking hands with the genial host. Everybody looked round,—the statesmen, the ballerina, the Yale men, and their happy enslavers,— wondering what illustrious Italian composer, or what not, they had just had the honor of dining with. Surely it could not be Verdi! The *tenore robusto*, at any rate, knew better than that. Could Crispi be studying American institutions *in muphti?*

"Good-evening, gentlemen," say the artist and the maestro, as they pass the door of the little room with bows and bland smiles.

"They speak excellent American!" quoth Tenterden. "Well, suppose we go, too. By the way, didn't you say that you had no overcoat? I believe I have an extra one at my rooms; suppose you call by and get into it,—provided, of course, you won't mind the color: it is nearly white, but you can get your own from your 'uncle' to-morrow."

It was but a short walk to Tenterden's "den," as he called it. Willis had never seen such rooms. And as comfort after comfort revealed itself, deeper and deeper grew his wonder that a man so placed should have found life unlivable.

Our own troubles, alone, are not to be borne. The poignancy, even of toothache, is dimmed, where it racks an alien jaw!

VI.

I THINK we shall have to pardon Mrs. Smithers. She had done her very best, and she had come, after a valiant battle, to the conclusion that if she did any better, she should surely burst.

Mrs. S. was seated in her parlor with Miss Wilkins, a maiden whom she had numbered among her boarders for ten or twelve years, and who had, during that period, reluctantly grown older by a couple of years or so. Her thin, narrow visage was hardly more than a frame for her big eyes,—eyes by which Miss Wilkins has set uncommon store ever since she received a certain note (now bethumbed and brown)—a certain little note (from a male) in which they—those eyes—were boldly classed among liquid orbs. For the rest, there was hardly enough·

of Miss W. to cover up her nerves, which a sudden mouse, even, was capable of totally upsetting.

The two women were alone.

A deep stillness reigned throughout the house from garret to cellar, broken only by the ticking of the clock. The deep, fresh snow muffled the sound of all footsteps of passers-by.

The clock struck twelve!

"My dear Mrs. Smithers, what *is* the matter? I never *heard* such a sigh,—that is, never since I—but no matter; let that pass."

The vast blue-veined lids slowly went down, veiling the light of the liquid orbs, as, with her transparent hand, she brushed aside the thronging memories. (While the note had been growing brown, the villain had married twice, and was the father of nine children.)

"For two or three days," continued she, "you are no longer your cheerful self."

" Cheerful self ! Ugh !"

Mrs. Smithers dropped back into her chair and closed her eyes; then suddenly sat up again, at the same time darting her hand into her pocket.

Something crackled there!

" Mrs. Smithers, what *can* be the matter ?"

" I feel that if I don't I shall burst; that's all !"

" Don't what ?"

. " Read that, Miss Wilkins. Read it aloud!"

Miss Wilkins, with eager, trembling fingers, withdrew the letter from the envelope, finding time to resolve, meanwhile, to advise the widow to accept the offer (it would be handy to have somebody to carve,—but who *could* it be ?), whether or not the aspirant ranked her eyes among liquid orbs. (Preposterous ! More like beads !)

" Mrs. Smithers, it is marked ' confidential.' "

"Never mind: read it," sighed Mrs. S., without opening her eyes.

"NEW YORK, Tuesday.

"DEAR MRS. SMITHERS:

"I owe you, this morning, two weeks' board. As I can see no reasonable prospect of paying you even this amount, I am resolved it shall not become greater. I leave your house, determined not to return till I have found employment——"

"Why, this is from Mr. Willis," said Miss Wilkins, glancing at the signature.

"Did you ever know a nicer, more lovable young man, Miss Wilkins?"

"But, my *dear* Mrs. Smithers, he is a mere boy!"

"What has that to do with it?"

Miss Wilkins was shocked. Like many women who have elected to pass their lives without partners, her mind was in a state of chronic exclamation over the matches made by her acquaintances. And now, here was Mrs. Smithers! Well, well, well!

"Doesn't that make the case all the sadder?" added that lady.

"Oh!" ejaculated Miss Wilkins, catching her breath; shying, like the young colt that she was, at the thought that she had so nearly uttered. She had been shocked; she was now startled, and read on, with unsteady voice:

"I take this step with the less shame, as my trunk, with its contents (I have left it unlocked), will more than cover my indebtedness. If I remain absent for ten days, you may take it for granted that I have been unable to find work in the city, and have gone elsewhere; and I hereby authorize you——"

"'Elsewhere,' Miss Wilkins,—'I have gone *elsewhere!*'"

"Oh, oh, oh!" half-shrieked Miss W., covering her face with her hands. How vividly she now recalled that the handsome young fellow had passed her the oatmeal in a very meaning way, more than once!

"Observe, Miss Wilkins, he does not say San Francisco—Chicago—the West: he says *elsewhere,—elsewhere,* Miss Wilkins!"

"Oo—ee—ee—ee!"

"I don't wonder that that word makes you shiver, Miss Wilkins." And Mrs. Smithers rose, and began to stir the fire nervously.

Miss W. felt lonely in her corner, and upset a heavy chair as she hastened to join her.

"Oh, how you frightened me!" cried Mrs. Smithers, letting fall the poker with a loud crash.

"Oh!" shivered, in reply, the pale lips of Miss Wilkins, as she clasped, with icy grip, the well-nourished arm of her friend.

"Do you believe in dreams, Miss Wilkins?"

"*Dreams*, Mrs. Smithers!" chattered Miss Wilkins, all eyes.

"Last night I dreamt—I dreamt I saw him——"

"We shall never see him more!"

"Oh, don't say that!—saw him stiff and cold, his hair——"

"His hair—his beautiful brown hair! Oh, me, me, me!"

."Yes, all wet—and—and matted, and——"

"WHAT'S THAT!!!"

The two women stood, pale and expectant, scarcely breathing. The jingle of keys was distinctly heard at the front door.

"Aren't all the boarders in?"

"All except—except—*him!*"

The jingling continued.

"Ugh!"

The obstinacy of front-door locks generally explains itself in accordance with what we know or believe of him who holds the key.

"Miss Wilkins, if my dream were true—

could—could—can *they*—you know-ow-ow—
use latch-ke-ke-keys ?"

"Oh, Lord, Lord, Lord !"

Tic, tac, tic,—jingle, jingle !

"And to think that we spent this evening,
of all others, at that wicked, wicked theatre !"
ejaculated Mrs. Smithers.

"Tic, tac, tic !

Miss Wilkins had been brought up at the
knee of a pious mother. Seeking, therefore,
to conjure away the dread vision of the
forest of many-twinkling, flesh-colored silk
tights evoked before her guilty soul by the
repentant cry of her friend: "*Now I lay me
down to sleep,*" she began, her hands clasped,
her liquid orbs upturned and glassy.

These words, so full of childlike faith,
seemed to suggest a line of defence to Mrs.
Smithers. At any rate, she made a spring at
the centre-table, and, seizing her family Bible,
clasped it, as a bulwark, against her vast and
motherly bosom. So she thought, at least;

but the truth of history compels me to admit that the buckler she bore was, in point of fact, none other than Webster's "great unabridged." Seeking what mankind loves to call "The Good Book," she got, in her haste, what is known to the advertising column as "The Best." Let it be pardoned unto her. For, as every fibre of her tingled with terror, and as she carried about her person an unusual number of fibres——

And Miss Wilkins, eager to be found standing upon the same platform with her friend, made a wild, slim dive for the prayer-book. In her swift swoop, however, she, too, missed her quarry. There she stands, her dazed eyes fixed upon a copy of Browning, opened upside-down,—a circumstance of no moment, by the way, in the case of that author——

Click!

Was not that the lock? Then why does not the door open? It *is* open, else why that icy draught?

Not a sound! Yes, another faintest of clicks! Then a stealthy tread!

Do THEY walk on tiptoe?

A form appears in the parlor door-way,—a form clad in an ulster almost white in itself, and now covered with snow; the lofty, raised collar of which overtopped the ears, while the skirts reached the ankles.

A beaming, rosy face, could one have seen it, and eyes glad with the gladness of expected welcome. But, to a prepared imagination, a spectre most gruesome!

The joyous greeting that was rising to young Willis's lips died unuttered. What could be the meaning of the amazing tableau that stood before him? His usually jolly landlady hugging the Great Unabridged to her rival bosom, and, with closed eyes, mouthing, with trembling lips, inaudible prayers! Miss Wilkins with bowed head, her liquid orbs, now dry with terror, bent upon the reversed pages of the Inscrutable One.

Our young friend had walked briskly, on leaving Tenterden's rooms, warmed without by his vast ulster, warmed within by gratitude and punch.   Ah, there were lights in the parlor; he could pay his bill before he slept! And now!

The fresh-hearted young fellow was shocked.   His heart sank within him. Even his voice sank, as he asked, in a trembling, guttural *basso profondo:*

"Ladies, don't you know me?"

Down fluttered Browning, down thundered the Great Unabridged; up rose two piercing shrieks!

And a Texan, who occupied a bed in the back parlor, thrust his hand beneath the pillow and waited, smiling grimly.   Wasn't that a woman's cry that awoke him!   No? I suppose I must have been dreaming.   Dash it, there *are* no burglars in New York!   And he nestled down again into his pillow, with a sigh.

VII.

"AND now," said Tenterden, as they lit their cigars after a late breakfast, "let's have your story. I do not ask from mere idle curiosity. It may turn out that, after hearing it, I shall be able to think of some way of aiding you without injuring myself."

"It will not take me long to tell it. At the close of the War of Secession, my father, though, like his neighbors, much crippled in his finances, still owned—at least he thought he did—a farm of twelve hundred acres of good land. But one fine day, a paper which he had signed as surety, many years before, 'merely as a matter of form,' and which he had almost forgotten, rose up and confronted him. This he met with a mortgage, and for five years struggled on, paying the interest with extreme difficulty. He succumbed at last, under the load, and died a broken-spirited man, leaving a widow and two children.

"My mother's courage rose with the emergency, and, with my assistance, though I was but a boy, we managed as well, if not better than during my father's lifetime. The mortgagee, too, being a friend of the family, was very lenient. But on his death, last year, his executors found that, contrary to expectations, his estate, too, was dreadfully involved. Nothing was left them but proceedings looking to foreclosure.

"It was immediately decided, in a council of war, that I should go straight to New York and seek employment, so that, when the crash came, I might be some sort of staff on which the family could lean. My sister, too, would have sought a place as governess, but my mother thought herself too old to fight the battle of life alone. So I was despatched to this great city, to make my way in the world, with almost the whole of my mother's little hoard in my pocket; and it was almost nothing.

"I came with a light heart, and with scarcely a misgiving; for a number of our acquaintances had removed to New York, after the war, and several of them had greatly prospered; and, as more than one of them had always professed to be warm friends of our family, I had no doubt that some one among them would put me in the way of finding something to do."

"My dear boy," laughed Tenterden, "you are truly delicious!"

"I was to be rudely awakened from my dream!"

Covering his eyes with his hand, he gave a little shiver. Presently he resumed:

"I would give anything in reason could I but erase from my mind the recollection of that frightful first week of mine in New York. Let me spare you—and myself—its details.

"One and all of these old friends of my people received me with bland smiles,—and —bowed me out of their offices with courteous regrets and kind suggestions. *How did the great West strike me?* For, it would appear, there was no room for another man in New York."

"A well-established *emigré* looks upon every new-comer as an impertinent interloper," remarked Tenterden, "who cheapens his success by assuming that it is possible for another."

"Yes, I know that now. But it was the last feather that broke the camel's back. The gentleman in whom I felt the greatest confidence I had not been able to catch at his office, as he came there rather irregularly, having practically retired from business. So I called at his residence. He had just finished his dinner, and received me in his dining-room, where he was smoking a thirty-cent cigar, with a decanter of sherry at his

elbow.   He was cordiality—hospitality, itself.
As I sipped his wine and puffed away at the
delicious Havana, and looked up into his soft,
brown eyes and handsome, benignant face, I
felt sure that here was a man who had the
leisure as well as the ability and the will to
find a place for me.

"He was the worst of the lot!   He would
not even listen to what I had to say; inter-
rupting me, at one time by filling my glass
with hospitable zeal, at another by urging
upon me a fresh cigar,—pointing out, with
his soft, fat, Sybaritic forefinger, the very best
one in the box.   Do you know, Tenterden,
as I descended that man's steps, that night,
and reached the street,—I could not help it,
—I just sobbed aloud!"

Tenterden rose from the table and walked
to and fro, once or twice, grimly swearing to
himself in a devout undertone; then, coming
to a halt in front of Willis: "Your benignant, cordial friend, with the flinty heart, was

an enigma to you, but I know his sort perfectly. They have reduced life to a science. They live by strictest rule. They are guided by one principle under all circumstances. And that principle is, never to give so much as one thought to the sorrows of their fellow-men. And, of all men, they alone are wise——"

Willis looked up.

"Of all men, they alone are happy, DAMN 'EM!" and his hand came thundering down upon the table. "And people are willing to live in such a world!"

"But there are some good people?" suggested Willis.

"Of course,—a pinch of salt, here and there, that saves humanity from general putrefaction. But don't listen to me: go on!"

"I think," resumed Willis, "that there was not one of the others but was annoyed, slightly, at least, at dismissing me without an effort to help me; but I believe that this bland gentleman had forgotten me before I turned the corner."

"Not the least doubt of it, and was therein wiser and happier than the others. Half-heartedness—in selfishness as in all things—is a mistake."

"After that, as my friends had abandoned me, I abandoned my friends. I threw myself upon the great public. I offered my services to firm after firm; but, as I was too bitter to give references, and acknowledged my inexperience, it might have been thought that I should never have gotten a place. But my very frankness actually procured me a situation, after a week's weary trudging up and down Broadway. But I brought my firm bad luck: they failed within a month.

"My second situation was as a street-car conductor. That I held only three days! You will blame me when I tell you how I lost it; but when I think of the highly dramatic close of my career in that direction, for the life of me——"

Thereupon, full of the joyous courage that new hopes give, Willis threw back his head; and his ribs, sustained now by a hearty and luxurious breakfast, began to shake with contagious vigor.

Tenterden's eyes twinkled in anticipation: "How was it? Tell me. I promise not to be too severe."

"Well, on the third day of my new employment,·who should enter my car but my friend who had overwhelmed me with sherry and cigars—and despair. A few blocks lower down, Mr. ——, one of New York's best-known millionaires, had entered my car. The driver had pointed him out to me, when my gentleman—and he was a gentleman——"

"Oh, there is no incompatibility between the character of a gentleman and that of a pig,—begging the pig's pardon."

"As soon as he espied the millionaire, he saluted him as though he were the most prized of friends, but getting a cool nod in return. As I watched him through the glass door, the servile adulation with which he hung upon the few curt words of the money-king filled me with shame and anger. And once, when the latter had dropped his glasses, and my man had stooped and handed them to him, with eager haste, the plutocrat almost sneered; for he could see that all this cringing was in honor of his money-bags. I dare say my friend would have been amazed, could he have known what were my feelings as I went forward to take his fare. I was ashamed to number him among my acquaintances.

"However, when he looked up: 'How are you?' said I. 'I beg your pardon,' said he, giving me a steady, stony stare. The millionaire looked from the one to the other of us, in surprise. My man felt it and colored.

'Don't you know me?' said I. I was no longer angry; but, very likely, my amused smile was not pleasant to him. 'I have not that honor,' said he. 'What,' I urged, 'you don't remember Bob Willis? nor "The Cedars?" Can't you recall the saddles of mutton, there, you used to think so fine?'

"Everybody in the car was listening, with open mouth. The magnate's eyes, peering intently over their glasses, seemed to burn the cheek of my friend of short memory. I must say he showed pluck in the way he looked me straight in the eyes. 'I can't say that I do,' said he."

"The cad!" broke in Tenterden.

"Here the millionaire put in his little oar: 'You seem to be under a singular hallucination, conductor?'

"I saw, at a glance, as our eyes met, that he was on my side. The fact is, he winked with his off eye.

"'Yes,' said I, 'and the hallucination is

somewhat strengthened by the fact that I spent the evening with the gentleman, recently. I can particularly recommend his cigars.'

"The plutocrat's eyes danced with merriment. The whole car tittered; for in New York, when one of our gods smiles, all of us common mortals laugh.

"Backed by so many millions, I was in exultant mood. I held out my hand. 'I have paid my fare,' snapped my man, fiercely. 'But won't you shake hands?'

"The well-lined ribs of the great man gently shook. The car guffawed. My victim wheeled aside with a snort, giving an anxious glance at the half-grinning face of his adored companion. Then I—it was dreadful, of course—it suddenly struck me as the very neatest thing possible, both to do and to say——"

"What was that?"

"'You won't *give* me your hand,' said I;

'but surely you won't mind *lending* me your nose!'"

"What!" shouted Tenterden. "Go on!"

"With that I leaned over and took his Burgundy-painted, prosperous proboscis between my thumb and forefinger——"

"Not really! IMMENSE!" roared Tenterden.

"I was almost laughing; I didn't wring it, exactly. You know how a dentist, with his forceps upon a molar, gives a quiver or so to his wrist—h'm?—just to let you know he is there?"

"DELICIOUS, by Jove! Here, waiter, two more *pousse-cafés!*" shouted Tenterden, beside himself. "What next?"

"The next thing in order would have been a fight; but just as my friend was rising, with the roar of a mad bull, an able-bodied young man arose and stood between us, who, laying his hand upon my shoulder, and exhibiting a shield, remarked, in a voice of authority, 'You are my prisoner!'"

" Were you taken to prison ?"

" Yes, but it was not a very serious affair;
for the officer laughed all the way down,
insisted on standing treat, and, somehow,
had me bailed out within an hour. He
would not tell me who went on my bond.
But, as I saw the millionaire hand him his
card, I had my suspicions.

" My examination, next morning, was
short and hilarious. My friend with the
short memory did not put in an appearance;
and the detective gave such an account of
the 'assault' that Judge McGuffy asked him,
with a wink trembling about the corner of
his eye, whether it seemed to him that I
had pulled it hard. Hearing that it was a
gentle tweak, and given with a smiling face,
'Whose face?' broke in the judge. 'The
prisoner's, your Honor.' 'Then it was a
joke,' said the judge, growing red. 'Sure,
your Honor !'

" Judge McGuffy drew himself up, and put

on a severely judicial air: 'Case dismissed. But look here, young fellow, don't you try it on again. This court' (and he winked in the direction of the reporters) 'don't appreciate such jokes. You ought to be ashamed of yourself. Next!'

"Of course I lost my place," added Willis, in conclusion.

"Is it possible?" laughed Tenterden; "merely for tweaking the noses of your fares to refresh their memories! But, my dear boy, it is clear to me that you can never hope to rise to eminence as a tram-way conductor. We must find some other career for you. How do you like city life? I dare say you would be glad to get back to farming, if the truth were known?"

Willis gave an eloquent look.

"Then I have a business proposition to make to you."

Tenterden stood for a little while with his hands in his pockets, then resumed:

"It so happens that I am a sort of agent, you might say; at any rate, I have control of a few thousand pounds belonging to an Englishman, which I am at liberty to invest, if. I see proper. You tell me that land is to be had cheap in Virginia, and a strong fancy has come over me to own a farm down there."

"Yourself?"

"I—I—well, I should have control of it."

"Of course."

"Now, I have been informed that my countrymen are often far from judicious in the purchase of land. I have heard of several among them who have come to grief, through—well, through knowing too much."

Willis smiled.

"Well, we have our weak points!" laughed Tenterden. "Now, I desire to do that rare thing,—profit by the experience of others. I shall place myself in the hands of a guide

and not rely on my British omniscience.
Will you assume that *rôle ?*"

Willis's eyes danced, but: "I am young
and inexperienced——"

"Yes, but you would know whom to call
in consultation. Moreover, the emoluments I
offer are far from splendid. I should pay your
expenses, and you might consider the sum
I have lent you a 'retainer.' In return you
would travel about with me and play mentor."

The young fellow found it impossible to
keep down the joyous smile that overspread
his face like morning light.

"And, should we buy a farm, you would
show me how to manage it for a year or so.
Is it a bargain? All right! Very well.
And it seems rather the natural thing that we
should look first at your mother's farm——"

"As to that——"

"Naturally,—but *I* have the right to
begin there. It might turn out that—however——"

" When are we to set out ? "

" Are you anxious to see that mother
and sister ?   Then why not write to-night ?
There is doubtless an inn in some neighboring village, where I—no ?   Oh, I understand—thanks, very much.   But let your
mother know that you are to bring a blasted
Britisher with you——   The Old Dominion !
Isn't that what you call it ?   They say you
are very hospitable down there, and that
Englishmen find themselves at home among
your people.   By the way, I suppose I shall
have to be a little careful as to forgetting
any one to whom you may introduce me—
your Virginian method of refreshing one's
memory——"

" Please forget that little episode——"

" Ah, but the simplicity and directness of
the thing !   Your hand—or your nose !
Delicious, by Jove !   Well, suppose we walk.
Nothing more ?   not even a pony ?—weed ?
—Ah ! "   .

VIII.

OUR two friends reached the front steps of "The Cedars" without being observed; for a cold wind whistled over the hills, and everybody was within-doors. But no sooner had the sturdy farm-horse sent up a burst of steam from his nostrils, in front of the sitting-room window, than one of its panes framed, for an instant, a lovely, eager young face. Then there was a lovely, eager young shriek of joy, the light pit-a-pat of hurrying feet, and the woosh-woosh of fluttering skirts——

What heart has not stood still at the sound, even though knowing that one's best sister was hundreds of miles away?

Open flew the door!

Parted, too, fair portals of pearls and of roses!

75

"Oh, Bob!"

Bob was flying up the steps, but his sister precipitated herself upon him with flushed cheeks and sparkling eyes,—with eager arms, and low, half-articulate murmurs of delight.

The love of a sister for a brother is beautiful as the morning.

After a responsive hug that would have done honor to a grizzly, Bob hurried to meet his mother; while his sister, finding herself confronted by the Englishman:

"We are *so* glad you came with Bob," said she, with a cordial hand-shake. And the honest greeting of her ingenuous eyes emphasized the hospitable warmth of her words and her manner.

Probably Tenterden, who had travelled in all parts of the world, lacked the normal amount of reserve with which his folk are credited. Whatever supply he possessed, however, melted instantly under the soft but steady light of those frank blue eyes,—delivered, too, at short range; for she did not stand at arm's length. Obviously, in her hospitable zeal, she remembered only that he was guest, she hostess.

"We are *so* glad you came with Bob!"

"So am I!" blurted out the Englishman, a trifle shocked, a moment afterwards, by his own bluntness; but, somehow, it seemed so natural to say that!

"Then we are *both* glad!"

Another laughing hand-shake. They were friends already!

Then, with a graceful stoop, she grasped her skirts in her right hand, with her left motioning him up the steps. The wind was whistling round her supple form. With a slight shiver she gave old Boreas the prettiest little frown,—enough to have made him ashamed of himself.

"You have on no wraps!" cried he, with sudden solicitude.

"No,—the sight of Bob——"

"Oh, but——"

And they trotted up the steps, side by side.

Aha!

Notwithstanding their reduced circumstances, the Willises dined late, in the belief that the consciousness that the day's labors were over could not but add zest to the simplest repast. A bright lamp, therefore, lit up the snowy damask, when our four friends took their seats at dinner on this cold December evening.

To Tenterden there was a certain pathos in the handsome appointments of the table, glittering remains of departed prosperity, as well as in the severe simplicity that marked the attire of the two ladies. As a man of the world he knew, and his rather painfully sympathetic nature made him feel, that it must be a sore trial to a pretty young girl to appear before a stranger in so economical a toilet. Though, why she should feel uncomfortable, on that account, mused he, I cannot see, for the life of me. It is the woman, not the dress, that we men care for. But you can't get that idea into their blessed little heads. I wonder if they are afraid of one another? That must be the trouble! There, didn't her hair flash prettily in the lamplight, as she turned her head!

Look to it warily, John Bull, lest she turn yours.

What a nice, little round table, and *la bella* opposite me! A loving family is a pretty sight. I wonder why there is so little affection in wealthy households? Too many gilded bones to fight over, I suppose,—that is, I "reckon." After all, things are tolerably even. What a tremendous swell the old lady is!—no, not swell, but one can see, at a glance, that she has had no end of grandmothers. And such a delicate, fine-grained skin! American women seem to me to surpass all others in that regard. There! that poor girl glancing down at her dress with a furtive sigh. Don't trouble yourself: I shan't look at it, as long as I have in full view those oval cheeks of rose-tinted ivory——

(Oho!)

"Thanks!"—how did she know I wanted the salt? But they all seem to know just what you lack, just a moment before you know it yourself. Deuced convenient kind of mind-reading, when a chap is as hungry as a wolf, and ashamed to ask for another slice. "Salt?"—and with such a pleasant, co—no, not coquettish, but—well, hospitable smile. It was not my fault, but the salt-cellar was so small that our fingers got entangled, and somehow we dropped it. However, not a grain was spilled.

I think pink finger-tips are very pretty.

Sometimes they are as soft as rose-petals.

What a capital idea these screens are! I had noticed that the doors and windows did not keep out the air very well. A few

f

pounds would make the house comfortable;
but I suppose they have not the pounds.
Deuced shame! But what a snuggery this
dining-room is! Bright fire on one side,
screens on the other three! Keeps out all
draughts and brings us all so close together.
Birds in a pie, by Jove! One feels as though
we were the only four people in the world,—
we and the old butler. Droll chap, this
Uncle Reuben: seems to think that I am
his guest! "Thanks, very much." Haven't
been here three hours; how is it that I feel
almost like one of the family?

(What!)

It must be the screens. Awfully snug,
I'm sure. Jolly fun, the way she pinched
Bob's ear, for teasing her.

Sisters are nice. I wish she—I mean I
wish I had a sister. Bob asked her whether
the old pouter-pigeon had been cooing
around lately. "A fat old widower, who"—
oh, I see—and she pulled his ear for calling

her an "unsophisticated squab." I have detested fat old widowers ever since I can remember. Come to think of it, they *are* like pouters,—strut, strut! Coo, coo! A friend of mine had a dovecot, and a burly old blue-rock widower made love to every female squab as soon as her bill broke the shell. Pig!

"Unsophisticated squab!" I wonder—h'm!

(Oho!)

X.

A FORTNIGHT later Tenterden had a conversation on business with Bob and his mother:

"Your son has informed you that I have come to Virginia with a view to investing a few thousand pounds of which I have control. I told him that, before looking elsewhere, I should examine into the expediency of buying the mortgage on your farm, which is to be foreclosed next month."

The widow gave a little shiver.

"I have seen your lawyer and acquainted myself with the facts of the case, and have ridden over every field on the farm in his company, as you know, to get some idea of its value. Bob recommended me to consult another lawyer, but I liked what I saw of your man of business,—and, besides, he is a farmer as well as a lawyer. After considering everything carefully, I have decided to invest for my English friend—with your consent, of course?"

The widow tried to speak.

Bob managed to say that the consent was a matter of course, since otherwise the family would be turned out of house and home. It would be a respite, at least.

Again the widow essayed to speak: "Oh, sir"—but could get no further; so, clasping her hands, she lifted up her eyes and her heart in passionate gratitude to that God who had long been her refuge and solace.

"You will understand," added Tenterden, interpreting her silence, "that this is a purely business transaction. I utterly disclaim all right to your thanks."

"But I must—I *will* thank you!" cried Mrs. Willis, smiling through her tears.

"Very well, I accept your gratitude gratefully," replied he, laughing. "But let us go into details. In England, as you know, the rate of interest is very low. My friend will therefore be satisfied with four per cent., on a safe investment. That will be a reduction of one-third."

"Oh, *thank* you!"

Tenterden shook a finger, smiling: "I thought——"

"Very well, I shall not interrupt you again."

"Four per cent., then. And hard enough you will find it to pay that. I have informed myself pretty well as to the profits of farming in this region. About all one can get out of it is a living."

The widow sighed assent.

"And if you can barely pay four, why promise six? I have discussed the matter with your lawyer, and he approves."

"I need hardly say that we do," laughed Bob.

"So much for proposition number one, and now for number two. I have said that, year in and year out, you will find it hard enough to pay interest at four per cent.———"

"Oh, we can easily manage that!" cried Bob, cheerily.

"I hope so; but, in regard to the coming year, I venture to predict that, with all the expense you will be at, getting things into shape, you will not be able to pay one dollar of interest!"

His two auditors looked shocked.

"Oh, I hope———" began Bob.

"Hope is all very well,—it is about all one ever gets, by the way; but, as I am not so sanguine, I have thought of a little scheme to meet the trouble."

Mrs. Willis and her son looked up, wondering. As for Tenterden, his manner was hesitating, and his clear, fresh, English complexion grew a trifle rosier as he began, turning to Bob:

"How would you like to take me as a pupil in farming?"

"A pupil in farming! You!"

"Why not? I am thinking of buying a farm—a little farm within my means—for myself—after a year or so; and, if I learned something· of the methods in use in these parts, before embarking in the business on my own account, wouldn't it lessen the probability of my being sold out? I am told that that has often happened to my countrymen. At any rate, this is my proposition: I will let you off with the first year's interest, in return for careful and systematic instruction in the art of farming."

"Systematic fiddlesticks! Absolutely absurd! Several hundred dollars for simply nothing!"

"You did not let me finish. I was going on to add that, if you thought I was paying too dear for your instruction——"

"Instruction!"

"Well, then, if it strikes you as so very ludicrous, suppose—you take me — as—a boarding pupil in your agricultural college? But," added he, hurriedly and with rising color, "I don't ask for an immediate decision. Wait till I return from Richmond. There is Uncle Rueben with the buggy. I must be off."

8*

XI

UNCLE REUBEN brought a note on his return from the station. As he entered the sitting-room, Bessie happened to be sitting next the door, and he handed it to her.

"What! so soon!" cried Bob.

"Come, Bob, come; you must not tease your sister."

"Pooh!" poohed the lovely Bess,—all the lovelier because of the conch-shell hue that flashed over cheek and brow.

"No, don't tease Little Missis, Little Mahster," chimed in the venerable Reuben, emboldened by long service and white hairs; "'case worriment sets folks ag'in' folks."

The implications of this sententious utterance made Bessie smile, in spite of herself.

"Why, Uncle Reuben, the note is not addressed," cried she, holding it up under his nose.

"No'm. De train ketch him a-studyin' and a-studyin' wid he head on he han', jess so; an' he didn't have no time to say howdy, nor good-by neither, on de outside o' de letter. He had to jump keen to git aboard, I· tell you. Howsomever, he fling some'n to ole Reuben, out'n de winder, he did, arter she were a-movin' pretty p'yert. He had time to think o' dat, h'ya, h'ya, h'ya!"

"But didn't he tell you whom the note was for?"

"I wonder ef he ain't done 'spress heself in de insides o' de letter? 'Cause my ole mahster, he writ me a letter, once, from de Springs, 'bout de craps; an' de governess-lady she read it to me, and 'pear like de bulk o' ole mahster's letter was de insides. Maybe——"

"Let us have the insides of the note, Bess: read it," laughed Bob.

"I WILL NOT!" And Elizabeth, bridling, tossed the letter to her brother: "It must be for you, *of course!*"

Whereupon, Uncle Reuben, with a deprecatory cough into his hand, stole from the room, softly closing the door behind him.

XII.

DURING the discussion of this note (and its author) between Bob and his mother, Bessie, with a copy of "The Newcomes" held in front of her face, seemed to be learning a favorite passage by heart.

"What do *you* say, Bess?"

"H'm?"

"H'm? H'm?" mimicked Bob; "you have not heard one word we have said, of course! Yet, to my certain knowledge, you have not turned a page for ten minutes!"

"It was not very respectful to mother to be watching me while she was talking," said Bess, reddening slightly.

"I forgive him, Bess. You heard what we said?"

"'M, ye-s. Wasn't it something about Mr.

Tenterden's making his home with us for a time ?"

"It was, you little humbug!" cried Bob, snatching at the book. The struggle ended in her stuffing it behind her back,—a place of safety, to the female mind.

"What do you want to know?" laughed she, in rosy triumph.

"Do you agree ?"

"Of course I agree! Do you suppose I would throw obstacles in the way of any business arrangements of yours or mother's ?"

"That isn't the question. Is the plan personally objectionable to you ?"

"Personally objectionable! Why should it be ?"

"Oh, I don't know. I had an idea that you did not like him."

"Not like Mr. Tenterden! And why, pray ?"

"You have never told me that you did."

Poor Bob!

XIII.

"Dis here fire feel mighty good. Wind was powerful p'yert, I tell you!" remarked Reuben, as he toasted himself before the kitchen fire.

"I believe you!" replied the cook. "So de gent'mun gone, is he? I always disremember he name."

"Temptin, Mr. Temptin, dat's what I hear 'em call him. Yes, he gone; but he'll be back Thursday. I'se to have de buggy at de train for him."

"What he give you, Reuben?"

"He gimme a dollar."

"Umgh!"

"Yes, he did. Here 'tis."

"H'm, brand new! Lemme hole it in my han'. Cert'n'y do crackle pretty! Reuben!"

"H'm? What de matter, Kesiah?"

"Who tell you dis was a dollar?"

"Who tell me? What kind o' fool question is dat, gal? I tell myself, in course! I know a dollar, jess as easy!"

"You does, does you! Is you notice dat quirlimikew on to de eend o' de note?"

"No, I ain't, an', what's mo', I ain't a-gwine to! Gimme back my dollar, 'oman! Mr. Temptin, he gimme a dollar, an' no quirlimikews can't make it no less! You wants to make me b'lieve dis is some o' dat little ole fractious cur'ncy as dey used to have, does you? Dis is a fifty-cent, I reckon! Maybe it's a quarter! H'm! next thing you'll call it a dime!"

"Dere ain't no call for you to git so ashy, Reuben. I jess ax you ef you see dat little quirlimikew in de cornder, an'——"

"Ashy! quirlimikew! Next time I git a dollar, I keeps it in my moneypu's'. Oh, I know; you mad 'cause he forgit you! Dat's it!"

"No 'tain't, nuther. He gimme jess de same, quirlimikews an' all." And with that, lifting the lid of her "chist," she thrust a crisp note under Reuben's nose.

"Den what for you go an' make small o' my belongin's?"

"I didn't no sich a thing!"

"Yes, you did!"

"I didn't, I tell you!"

"You did!"

"Hello, hello! What are you old people quarrelling about?" cried Bob, cheerily, as he thrust his head into the kitchen door.

"Dat you, Little Mahster? I glad you come; you can settle a p'int twixt Kesiah an' me. She ax me what de gent'mun gimme when I druv him over, an' I say one dollar; an' den Kesiah, woman-like, she must hole it in her han'; and den, 'stid o' han'in' me back my dollar, she set her head fust on one side an' den on t'other, she did, an' spy at my dollar; an' den she upped, she did, an' said 'twarn't no dollar.   Ain't dat a dollar, Little Mahster?"

Little Mahster took the note in his hand. The heated disputants hung upon his looks with bated breath.

He raised his eyes to Reuben's face, then slowly shook his head: "No, that is not a dollar-bill!"

"What I tell you?" cried Kesiah.

Poor Reuben's eyes fell.   His stature shrunk half a foot.

A negro does not care for money, as such, but is acutely sensitive to the ignominy of defeat.

Lifting his hand to his head, the unhappy old butler toyed feebly with the snowy fringe of hair that shaded his ears:

"What is it, den, Little Mahster?" asked he, in a humble whisper.

"It is a five-dollar bill."

"Glory!" cried Kesiah,—"he gimme jess sich another!"

Bob looked thoughtful as he walked back, slowly, towards the house. He stood for two minutes with his foot on the lower front step.

"Why that brown study?" asked Bessie, throwing up the window.

"Oh, nothing!" replied Bob.

XIV

"WELL," said Bob, a few days later, at breakfast, "this is Thursday."

"Thursday?" repeated Bess, looking up; "what of that?"

"Why, Tenterden will be back this afternoon."

"Oh!"

"Had you forgotten it?"

"N-no,—not forgotten it, exactly. I thought that perhaps you were reminding us that to-night will be Christmas-eve."

"Ah, Christmas-eve!" repeated Bob, a smile chasing away the shade of annoyance wrought by his sister's indifference to his friend. "Have you been able to get the eggs, Bess? Plenty and fresh? Good! And, mother, I hope some of the old cognac is left still? A little of the peach-brandy

too! Ah, we shall have an old-time eggnog!
I hope he will like it."

"Who?" asked Bessie; and the little finger of her right hand, as she raised a fragile
cup to her bewitching mouth, curved itself,
unconsciously, into a rosy interrogation-
point.

"Why, Tenterden, of course!"

"Oh!"

Bob laid down his knife and fork, with an
impatient gesture, then resumed his breakfast in silence.

"Why, what's the matter, Bob? What's
the matter? Tell me," repeated she, laying
hold of his chin and pulling his head round
till their eyes met. "Why, mother, he is
positively angry!"

"No, I am not angry; but, as Tenterden
is to live with us for a year, it is a pity that
you should begin by disliking him, that's
all."

"Disliking him! The silly boy!" And,

dropping her hands upon the table, Bessie's eyes appealed to the ceiling.

"Mother, do I dislike Mr. Tenterden?"

"Not that I know of, my dear. At any rate, you said, the day of his arrival, that you thought him exceedingly handsome."

"Did I?" There was a faint flush on her cheek. Witnesses are sometimes overzealous. "What I meant was, *tolerably good-looking.*"

"He is thundering handsome," broke in Bob, aggressively.

"Oh, *you* are *in love* with him!"

"Bess, why don't you like him? Tell me?"

"How often must I repeat that I like him [sip of coffee] ever [sip] so much? Would you have me dying in love with the poor man, before he knows the color of my eyes, very likely?"

"Speaking of color, Bess, your walk this morning seems to have brought the roses to your cheeks. Upon my word, if any fellow except your brother saw you, the way you are looking now———"

"Flatterer!" and she gave his ear a grateful pinch. "Well, I must go and get through with my practising early to-day."

"Mother, didn't you notice what a lovely color her walk gave her?"

Poor Bob!

XV

"WELL, I done fotch him back, Kesiah, an' glad un it, at dat!"

"Course you glad! I too! Bound I was at de kitchen do' to curchy to him! He see me, too, an' he bow back at me. He is quality, ef you hear Kesiah, Mr. Tenpin is!"

"Tenpin! Tenpin! What for you keep resistin' on callin' de gent'mun out o' he name? Ain't I done tell you he call heself Temptin?"

"Lor', Reuben, I neber could 'member none o' dem outlandish, furrin names!"

"Wuss and wuss, gal! Don't you know Mr. Temptin ain't no furriner?"

"I hear 'em say he come from furrin parts."

"What sort o' furrin parts! Ain't he tell me, heself, he come from ole Englunt? An' hukkum he talk ole Fidginny talk ef he war one o' dese outlandishers? Ain't I hear 'em at de depot, on de trains? Sich another cacklin' like hens, an' gruntin' like pigs, an' squawkin' like crows! Lor', chile, you don't know nothin', settin' back here in dis here kitchen! One day dey jabber dat foolish dat I upped an' said to de depot gent'mun, says I, 'Ef dey *is* folks, why don't dey talk like humans? Fust thing dey know,' says I, 'some o' dese here circus people gwine to catch 'em, an' den whar is dey? In de cages wid de show critters an' rangytangs an' varmints.' B'fo' Gaud, I tell him jess so, an' he laugh an' laugh, twell he 'most buss he wesscoat!"

Kesiah (after putting some strain on *her* wesscoat): "I don't reckon Englunt is so ve'y fur from here, arter all?"

"Kesiah, jess lemme give you a p'int 'bout dat; people who is fur is furriners, jess like people who ain't fur ain't furriners. Nothin' c'yant be no plainer'n dat!"

"Cert'n'y, dat's a fac'."

"Reuben don't drive to de depot, an' mix wid de people, for nothin'!"

"B'fo' Gaud, Reuben, ef you goes on in dis way, one o' dese days you'll know more'n you don't know! Howsomever, I hear one o' dese little school-niggers say dat betwixt Fidginny and Englunt dere was de most owdaciousest big ribber as ever was. He 'lowed as how de name of it was a Notion, or some'nornurrer. How 'bout dat?"

"Notion don't sound so monstrous big! I bet you 'tain't a tetchin' to Jeames Ribber? An' whar's de bridges, leastwise ferry-boats? Howsomever, he here, Notion or no Notion. Whar must we hide all dem Christmas things he fotch along? In de dairy? He want to s'prise 'em, you see. Dere is a hamper o' wild ducks an' pattridges an' things, an' a basket o' fruit, an' another basket o' champagne——"

"Heish!"

"An', Lor' bless my soul, I neber see so many bandanas in my born days,—a whole bunch un 'em, ef my name's Reuben!"

"Bound he fotch a diamond ring or a necklace, leastwise some powerful fine ornament, for Little Mistiss?"

"What kind o' foolishness you talkin', Kesiah! De quality don't 'cept jewelry an' sich, onless dey engaged!"

"Maybe not! Maybe not! Howsomever, when I was a gal, I always used to 'spise a beau, 'cep'n' onless he were givvy! An' I do reckon gals is gals!"

"He fotch Little Mistiss some flowers. I see de eends a-stickin' out o' de paper."

"Flowers! Lord 'a' mussy! White folks is cuyous, to-be-sho! Gimme a p'yar o' shoes, or a hankcher, or a dress to wrop myself up in! No flowers for Kesiah! Here to-day, an' gone to-morrow! Reuben, does Mr. Tenpin—I should say Tentpin—want Little Mistiss, you reckon?"

"Want her? He want her powerful! He
needn't try to fool Reuben, f'all he come
from Englunt. 'Howdy do, Uncle Reuben?'
[mimicking]; 'an' how's Mrs. Willis, an'
how's Mr. Bob?'—makin' 'ten' he done forgit
Little Mistiss! Nemmind! Ole Reub got
he eye on you! I been see de quality pro-
jickin' 'long o' dey lady-loves afore dis!
Presen'y, fixin' up he mouf, sort of prim-like,
an' lookin' way 'cross de field, like he warn't
a-keerin', 'an' I hope Miss Willis [mincing]
is quite well?' 'Miss Willis!' You jess
ought to hear how he renounce her entitle-
ments! Soft an' easy! Butter wouldn't melt
in he mouf! Fool Reuben? He may be
Englunt, but dis here [slapping his breast]
is ole Fidginny! Umgh—umgh!"

"An' ain't I see how she look when she
see him come back?"

"I ain't see her nowhar!"

"Course not! You ain't fling you eye up
to her window. A 'oman knows whar to

look for another 'oman. Ain't I see her jess a-pullin' back her curtains, sly as a weasel, an' a-peepin' down wid one eye, an' a-leanin' over an' watchin' twell he git into de house; an' ain't I see glory on her face?"

"You did! Well, ef she *is* lookin' towards him, she done fool Reuben,—an' Little Mahster too. She make Little Mahster mad, she talk so keerless-like 'bout he friend. Howsomever, Mr. Temptin better watch he-self, f'all you see glory shine in her eye, for I hear 'em say dat a Fidginny gal is de most flirtinest critter dat ever war wropped up in ten yards o' calico!"

"Umgh—umgh! Go 'long, man! Don't talk! Ain't I see 'em myself?"

XVI

"You must not listen to Bob's raptures," said Bessie; "eggnog is wretched stuff,—at least I think so,—but it is fun to make it."

"You will let me help, won't you?"

"Can you beat eggs?"

"I don't know, I'm sure; I never tried."

"How education must be neglected in England!"

"I have come to Virginia to complete mine!"

Six or eight of the neighbors were expected to take part in the Christmas-eve festivities. Among these was a certain Miss Geoffrey. Bob sketched her, for Tenterden's benefit ("Forewarned is forearmed, you know!"), under a shower of laughing protests from his mother and sister.

According to Bob, Miss Judith Geoffrey

110

was a young thing not far from forty ("Oh, Bob!"), — well, thirty-nine, then, — whose bright black eyes had, from all accounts, been bewitching, twenty years ago ("Robert! Robert!"); indeed it was no secret that they subjugated, at about that prehistoric period, "the Pouter." (Delighted smile from Tenterden.) But he, finding her obdurate, had married her cousin, who had died years ago, leaving one child,—a son. In fact, there were few young men of her time, in the county, who had not, more or less, succumbed to her fascinations.

But she was Miss Geoffrey still.

The ill-natured whispered that this was because a certain man had failed to come to the point. However, whether from disappointment or from inborn tendencies, Miss G. had come to be one of those women who shed unmerited reproach upon the name and estate of "old maid." Her once bright black eyes had grown to be hard, glittering, restless interrogation points,—perpetually searching, yet never finding any good thing. Recognizing the fact that human faculties were limited, and that no one mind can grasp all things, Miss Judith Geoffrey had learned to confine hers to meditation upon the faults and follies of her friends, and, seizing the idea that too much must not be exacted of one poor little tongue, she had long since restricted the activity of hers to this one field.

But how can news be either gathered or spread abroad, if one be not up and a-doing? Her mother's carriage-horses were fat and lazy; so the daughter possessed herself of a fiery little black mare, as tireless as her own tongue; and, mounted upon "Termagant," gathered gossip at a gallop, and dispensed it for miles around.

Matters matrimonial were her specialty,— and it was roundly asserted that she had disapproved of more matches than anybody. If a swain from the next county found favor in the eyes of a daughter of one of her neighbors, 'twas she who was first to hear, for example, that the State Insane asylum was populous with his relatives. And should a young man of the neighborhood seek a bride elsewhere, earliest of all did her thin lips raise the lament that he should think of a narrow-chested girl, all whose narrow-chested sisters already filled consumptives' graves.

She was to be met at all social reunions,—dread of her tongue standing her in the stead of desire of her society. And no one enjoyed these festive occasions more than she, for she was human—manly, almost—in her thorough appreciation of the solid comforts of life. Yet the vigor with which she attacked the dainties in which she delighted did not, in the least, mar the perfection of her life-work. For so nimble was her well-trained tongue, that it knew how, even from the *inopportuno loco* of a mouth full of chicken-salad, to shed disastrous criticism upon the hostess who had compounded it.

It remains but to add that she was known exclusively, among the young fellows of the vicinage, by the *nom de guerre* of *Mrs. Geoff's Judy.*

"Oh, I don't fear the redoubtable Judy," laughed Tenterden. "She will never be able to find out anything about me or my relatives!"

"Don't be too sure of that!" said Bob.

"To genius all things are possible!" added Bessie.

XVII.

The craunching of wheels was heard. Bob went to the window.

" The Pouter !"

" Mr. Edmondson is one of our most prized neighbors," explained Mrs. Willis, with all the gravity she could muster.

" He sets great store by some of us !" said Bob, looking hard at his sister ; but she, busy with her work, did not seem to hear. So Bob curvetted across the room with puffed cheeks and inflated chest ; and, bringing his lips close to her ear : " Coo ! Coo-oo !"

Bessie pushed him away, half amused, half angry ; and he hurried out to meet the guest. A capital mimic, thought Tenterden.

Back rushed Bob, presently, thrusting his head in at the door :

" I say, Bess, he has brought Tommy !"

"Bob is perfectly outrageous!" and she swept from the room.

No matter how absurd the admirer of a woman may be, she would have the monopoly of laughing at him.

"Confound the old chap!" thought Tenterden; "surely she can't—ah—like him?"

"I wonder," mused Edmondson, as he climbed down from his groaning buggy, "what kind of a looking fellow is that long-legged Englishman that I hear Bob has picked up?"

The hurrying of undisciplined yet confident footsteps was heard in the hall. A BOY invaded the parlor: "How d'ye do, Mrs. Willis? How d'ye do, sir? You are the Englishman, I reckon. I don't know your name. My name is Tommy Edmondson."

"And mine is Tenterden, at your service, Master Tommy!"

"I am glad to know you, Mr. Tenterden!"

"Thanks, awfully. I reciprocate, I'm sure."

Mrs. Willis looked embarrassed. Not so Tommy Edmondson. Planting himself squarely in front of Tenterden, he looked him over with rapid eye and startling self-possession.

His father made a companion and equal of our sturdy young friend, and took him about with him everywhere,—a practice, as some suggested, that possibly had something to do with his chronic difficulty in supplying the late Mrs. Edmondson's place. Without doubt Tommy was, as a specimen, as a sample, disquieting. His bold eye, his ready initiative in conversation, his freckle-spangled nose, that tilted so high its flaunting nostrils as to make the beholder feel himself almost a witness of the operations of his mind,— these were traits not likely to inspire a longing to be his step-mother.

Tommy belonged to the pervasive species of boy. When he was in it, the largest house was choke-full of boy from garret to cellar. He swarmed over the stairs, he leaned out of every window, his voice was heard in the halls thereof. And his fond parent, by incessantly quoting him, multiplied him as mirrors do an audience. Yet, far from being a bad fellow, could he but be reduced in number. A cube root of him had been tolerable.

In one singular regard the relations between himself and his father were unique. Tommy could not remember his mother, and was a hearty ally of his surviving parent in his various attempts to find her successor: 'Darn a house without a woman in it!' was a favorite apothegm of this philosopher of thirteen summers.

They freely discussed together all possible candidates; and Tommy, an admirer of the sex at large, rarely blackballed any of his father's nominees. But he resolutely drew the line at Mrs. Geoff's Judy. Whenever Mr. Edmondson, weary of his fruitless pursuit of sweet young graduates, showed symptoms of returning to his first love: "There is not a house in the United States big enough to hold both her and me," quoth Tommy.

"Perhaps she would not take me, Tommy!"

"Take you ain't the word! She'd snap you up quicker'n a trout would a minnow; though you don't look much like a minnow, do you, Pop?"

Tommy was right, if humoristic to the verge of disrespect. Mr. E. did not remind one of a minnow. To draw him at one stroke, imagine a man who had adjusted over his person, at the junction of vest and trousers, a mammoth inverted finger-bowl, as it were. There and there only had nature banked up the adipose tissue.

This involved a peculiarity of carriage which gave him out as a man of extreme hauteur; whereas the honest gentleman was merely obeying the laws of equilibrium.

Poor man, he was hardly on cordial terms even with his own coat; which, resting upon his shoulders, merely, dangled free of his back.

It remains to add that his cheeks, rosy and shining, stood out like the pouches of a ground-squirrel when stuffed with acorns.

Such were Tommy and his Pop,—the first of the Christmas-eve guests to arrive.

A light step was heard in the hall, and Bessie tripped into the room, a vision of youthful grace and beauty.

The Pouter bounded from his chair; beaming, breezy, impetuous as Romeo,—every inch a widower!

Younger than youth he seemed,—lighter than a feather!

"Lordy, just look at Pop!"

And, after a burst of admiring laughter, the dreadful boy stood close against the couple, mouth agape, legs wide-spread, hands in pockets,—drinking in every word. Under his father's vivacious and gallant sallies his big mouth seesawed in sympathy, his pert little pug nose joyously twinkling, wrinkling, —diving, at times, almost out of sight under the freckles, like a shore-crab beneath the sand. Tommy idolized his father. Every neatly-turned compliment he saluted with an applauding grin; and his bright, dancing eyes said, as plainly as eyes could, "This is what I call courting!"

"The Pouter is heavily handicapped," rejoiced Tenterden.

The situation was strained. Bessie was on thorns. Her face tingled; and, at last, glad of any excuse, she rushed madly into the hall, and imprinted an effusive kiss upon the cold and bitter lips of Mrs. Geoff's Judy.

XVIII.

It was nine o'clock. The expected guests had all come. It was time to begin the egg-nog; and the little party rose merrily, to betake themselves to the dining-room,—Mr. Edmondson and Bessie in the van.

There are widowers and widowers.

This one makes frequent and lachrymose allusions to the late Jemima, poor thing! To sympathizing ears he pours out his grief, in retired nooks, on secluded sofa. And poor, poor, little Gladys, darling lamb, must grow up, alas, without a mother's care!

To widows, to maids long since bereft of hope, to the plain sisters who never nourished any, pipes he his sad refrain.

He is hurt—shocked—at the merest hint that the sea is big, and not without fishes still. Poor, poor Jemima! Ah, never, never, never more!

Trust him not, sad-eyed grandmother of little Gladys! Your bereaved son-in-law is already peeping forth wistfully, through his tears. He belongs to the still-hunting class of inconsolables,—using the dear departed as a stalking horse. Sad—that her recent demise should mar the hilarity of his coming nuptials!

Far other was our rotund friend, Tommy's Pop. No still-hunter, he; no wary wolf darkly stealing upon the unsuspecting fold, the sweetly-bleating ewe lambs. Comparable, rather, to the bereaved dominie,—swiftest of mortals to seek consolation; or to the meteoric hawk,—dropping from the clouds, —and loud is the cackle of pullet and of hen!

Yes, Pop was a marrying man. His contempt for single-blessedness was even boisterous. He wanted a wife. Tommy wanted him to have a wife. And a wife he would have.

He was absurd, if you will. But he was not a fraud.

Tenterden smiled, beholding the springiness of his step, his jaunty carriage, the cajoleries of his widowed eye, as he escorted Bessie to the dining-room. It made him feel old, the ruddy smile of this amazingly youthful rival.

"Coo-oo!" breathed Bob into his ear.

And Mrs. Geoff's Judy, turning, gave the two young men a look of grim wonder. How could people laugh in a world where a fat old fool was permitted to make love to a silly young girl!

Have you forgotten, Judy, that you too once were young and silly? Or do you remember it only too well?

XIX.

Upon the table a pyramid of snowy eggs in a trim basket; a great ancestral bowl; a broad blue-china dish. And, upon the sideboard, a jug of cream and a bottle or so.

"Ah," cooed the Pouter, rubbing his hands, rocking gently from heel to toe, and flashing upon the company a smile rubicund and cheery.

"Pop knows what's good!" ejaculated innumerable Tommy, caressing his parent with an admiring glance.

Bessie now disappeared into the pantry, and presently emerged, smiling, and veiled in an apron from chin to ankle.

Intellectual maidens are constantly upbraiding us men because we do not know, poor things, what kind of a girl we want. It is so silly of us, they justly urge, to go mad over rosy cheek, merry eye, dimpling smile, trim ankle. Fading flowers these,—while culture-talk would go on forever! I am at my wit's end, therefore, trying to find an excuse for the young Britisher. When he saw Bessie briskly bustling about the table, the light of hospitable zeal upon her sweet face, and that *darling* apron (the great, silly six-footer!) trying its best, and in vain, to hide the undulating perfections of her supple figure——

And she, poor girl, had put on her best dress, that evening! It had been her best for ever so long! But it *was* her best,—and she was chagrined to have to hide it, even for a time——

Virgins, ye know not the day nor the hour!

"What a womanly air it gives her, that blessed apron,—smooth, cool, shining, freshly ironed! [Pooh-pooh! to thee, degenerate son of Albion!] How she would grace a

house of her own! Ah me, if only—how
that old idiot smirks! How neatly she
cracks the shells upon the rim! [*sic !*] What
a little house-keeper she would make! What
a home! I wish she would wear it always!
Damn that Pouter!" [Oh, fie!]

For Bessie had just put that gentleman in
charge of the broad dish. He, being an acknowledged adept in making eggnog, was to
beat the whites, she undertaking the yolks in
the big bowl.

Before striking a blow, she tucked up the
sleeve of her best dress above the elbow.
And in an instant the poor apron was forgotten! And no wonder! That arm, snowy,
smooth, creamy-soft,—its plumpness suddenly shrinking into a round, blue-veined
wrist! And that firm little fist, grasping the
spoon, and making merriest muffled clatter
among the golden yolks! And those mobile
lips pursed up into daintiest pucker of house-
wifely zeal! Like crumpled rose-petals!

And first the fair head dropped on this shoulder, and then on that, as she bent herself to her task; and the yellow foam rose higher and higher, above the rhythmic splutter of the spoon. And sometimes she steadied her resolution by pressing beneath snowy teeth that saucy rosebud of an under lip!

And more than once there came, from very earnestness, the prettiest little frown, that drew together her brows above the azure of her eyes,—like two pencilled clouds above bits of sky.

And every now and then, to her companion in the merry toil, a sociable, encouraging smile,—as though she asked, "How are you getting on?"

The Pouter beamed!

At last, "Look!" cried he.

"Oh, don't try that to-night!" Pleaded she; "it might——"

But, grasping his dish at either end, the

Marrying Man, with a quick motion of his wrists, inverted it. There was a pretty little shriek from the ladies, followed by murmurs of applause, as they saw the snowy peaks of the mimic mountains pointing downward yet holding fast. He did that every Christmas-eve, and always under protest,—for once there had been an avalanche upon the table.

The Pouter replaced the dish upon the table, with a bow and a smile of modest triumph.

"I tell you what," burst out Tommy, with conviction, and glancing up at Bessie, "when it comes to beating up eggs, Pop's a honey-cooler!"

A universal shout of laughter greeted this enigmatical panegyric. Even grim Judy smiled. As for Bessie, she let drop her spoon among the frothing yolks, while tears of merriment bedewed her flushing cheeks. For it was obvious to her, as to all, that poor Tommy was pleading his father's cause.

i

"A what!" gasped the Englishman.

Bob threw up his hands in despair. His ribs were shaking so that he could not explain that this pet expression marked the high tide of Tommy's approval,—the foam on the crest of the wave of his admiration.

"You must not use slang, Tommy," replied the fond parent, patting his offspring's shaggy crown.

"Do you know, Bessie," remarked Mrs. Geoff's Judy, in a stage-whisper illustrated by a galvanic smile, "I heard Tommy apply that same droll epithet to you, as he and his father came out of church, last Sunday? How nice that *he* should think his father and yourself a *pair* of—what was it?"

"Oh, very!" replied Bess, damming up, with an adverb, a sudden tide of wrath.

It was now time to mix in the sugar,—a spoonful to each egg. Bessie stirred, while a fair young neighbor (fairer even, Bob thought, than Bess. Brothers are often so impartial!) agitated a spoon above the deep bowl. Everybody has to help make eggnog. Bessie's spoon grew heavier each moment:

"Oh," cried she, gracefully collapsing, with a look of plaintive fatigue,—"ah, you want your lesson, now? Take the spoon and let us see what you can do!"

But how was he to take it? She could not lay the spoon down, for its bowl was covered with the sugared yolk; the handle she grasped in that dimpled little fist.

"*There!*" said she, withdrawing her hand from within his with a rosy, apologetic little smile,—as though she said, There was no other way!

Tenterden liked the way well enough. When that soft little hand, smooth as satin, glided from within his grasp, releasing to him the spoon——

With a few laughing directions, Tenterden was not long in getting the hang of the thing. Then his rival began slowly the transfer of the contents of his dish into Tenterden's bowl. Then the cream, followed by the cognac; poured in, each, in a delicate, trickling stream. Then a gill of the wonderful " old peach," redolent of the orchard. And, over all, the brown dust of nutmeg.

The eggnog is done,—and upon the air a comforting harmony of savors floats!

The Pouter had for years acted as master of ceremonies during these Christmas-eve frolics at The Cedars. As I have poked a little fun at him, it is only fair to say that a kindlier man or a truer gentleman it would be hard to find. · Though his waste of waist did make him stand at some distance from the bowl, he presided over it with graceful hospitality and a charming warmth of manner. His bow and his smile, as he ladled out the nectar to his rival, and his few quiet but cordial words of welcome to the county, over their chinked glasses, quite won the young Englishman.

"How do you like it?" asked Bessie, seeing him approach the corner where she stood. "Wretched, don't you think so?"

"On the contrary, it is delicious!"

"I am so glad you like it! At any rate, it is good fun to make it."

"The beverage itself," replied he, tapping his glass, "is delicious,—but making it was—heavenly!"

Bessie flushed—just a little. Oh, they know!

12

THE winter passed swiftly away. When spring came, Tenterden was to fall to, under Professor Bob. Meantime, he was a sort of a professor himself. He was a fair pianist; and, hanging idly about the house, while the cold winds whistled over the fields, it had been selfish not to have offered to help Bessie with her music.

Selfish! Not he! On the contrary, he was ever so kind. He gave Bessie a lesson every day. In one respect he showed, for so young a professor, judgment of a high order. He did not, as the injudicious do, insist on his lovely pupil wearing out her rosy little fingers, thumping, thumping, unceasingly. He gave her many little breathing spells, allowing talk,—which is, to a young woman, I understand, a form of rest.

134

Sometimes Mrs. Willis would think, as she sat in her room, sewing, that the lesson had been over, half an hour; when, suddenly, a chord would burst upon her ear.

"Why don't you let poor Mr. Tenterden give you the lesson and be done with it?"

"Oh, he has to explain, you know! I am sure he must think me awfully stupid."

"I dare say," said Bob. "At any rate, it takes you two hours, sometimes, to understand a few bars. Explaining the theory, no doubt."

"The theory of what?" asked Mrs. Willis, half smiling, as she took aim at the eye of a needle.

"Upon my word, mother, nothing of the kind goes on. He never talks any—non-sense—not one word,—honestly, Bob!"

"All right, Elizabeth! You ought to know. Perhaps he does not talk any nonsense; but he *looks* lots of it." Whereupon, Bob, heaving a portentous sigh, cast upon his sister the dismal glance of a despairing lover.

"Poor, silly, old Bob!" exclaimed Bessie, pouncing down upon the offender and cruelly pinching his cheeks, then sealing his forgiveness with inarticulate murmur of laughing yum-yums.

There are ways and ways of being silly old Bobs!

Fibbing on certain points is the inalienable right of woman. But what Bessie had said was, in a literal sense, at least, quite true. So far as mere words went, the young Englishman had not talked any "nonsense." Why, I know not; for I am not of the omniscient school. But it did not matter. She knew and rejoiced. Perhaps she might have preferred the spoken words. But even silence may be eloquent.

Not English is needed, nor French; nor, lingo of love, Italian; impotent devices, all! For, in the young days of old, the warm waves of the Ægean, wondering at their lovely burden, bore foam-born Venus to the shore. And she, lying, rosy, upon the golden sands (for sofas were not), smiled when wooing zephyrs came and toyed with her wondrous hair,—smiled when the saucy wavelets, creeping up a-tiptoe, beat, creamy-soft, against her infinite perfections!

And, dimpling, she beckoned to her side (for Satan, even then, had mischief for idle hands to do)—beckoned to her side the nightingale, and taught him how to trill; taught the turtle-dove to make moan; whispered to young men and maidens the sweet mystery of sighs, of starts, of eloquent eyes, —of tell-tale cheek, of snowy, quick-beating bosom; revealed the universal language— the volapük of love!

12*

XXI

FEW occupations afford such endless opportunities for falling in love as that of amateur professor of music. It is through the eyes, for the most part, that the poison enters, as is well known; and what better chance could one have of feasting them unobserved! Tenterden is entitled to our sympathy, such as it is:

The lissome figure before him, swaying now to the right, now to the left; the cunning fingers scampering in mad frolic, up and down, or else clinging lovingly to loving tones; the fair young head bent forward, now in earnest scrutiny, now thrown back in half-disdainful triumph; the blue eyes at one time darkening in sympathy with the fervid majesty of the song,—again, rapt, dreamy, sweetly disconsolate, dissolved in tuneful woe!

And if, sometimes, she would turn and face him, pouting and reproachful, her hands fallen despairingly in her lap, and demand in pitifullest accents, *how* could he expect her to make that *horrid* run,—could a professor do other than show her the fingering? And, even though she leaned over, ever so far, to give him room while he struck the notes, how was she to get entirely away from his shoulder?—You forget how very broad they were. And if his left hand sprang an octave downward, looking for the base, must she not raise her round arm out of his way? And what was there, then, to protect her waist from the transient pressure of his bashful wrist? Upbraid the composer, rather, who wrote the music that way.

But how on earth was she, bending farther and farther away from him, how was she to see what his fingers were doing? But he was patient and good, and showed her, again and again, without one scolding word. Once, indeed, he did seize a wayward, cantankerous finger, that would persist in striking all awry, —did seize the giddy little thing, and bend it down on B flat—*there!*—but he said it more in sorrow than in anger.

And she, letting fall her right hand listlessly by her side, and with her left elbow resting upon the piano—propping upon her thumb her saucy chin, raised her eyes to his: "Don't you think I am the stupidest girl in the world?"

And the warm, fragrant breath, bearing upward the soft words from dewy lips, floated about him—an intoxicating mist!

XXII.

THE winter that was now past had been one of unalloyed happiness to Tenterden. He had come to Virginia with no fixed intentions. Mere restlessness and a strong liking for Bob had been his sole motives. But he had found a charming home.

The neighbors, too, had been kind. He knew them all for miles around. There had been many unpretentious but jolly dinners, some dances, and eggnoggings galore; at all of which he had been made to feel entirely welcome. And nowhere did he feel more at home than under the roof of his rival, Mr. Edmondson, whom—simply for the innocent entertainment of the reader, and without the least satiric intent—I have dubbed The Pouter. True, Edmondson did not know, as the reader and I do so well, that the young

Englishman had fallen a victim to Bessie's fascinations; only, he could not see how he could possibly have avoided it. At any rate, he felt, instinctively, that he had in Tenterden a formidable rival.

But Edmondson was such a good fellow, and was, moreover, so impenetrated, to his very marrow, with the spirit of hospitality, that, when once a man was under his vine and fig-tree, he, like an Arab whose salt you have tasted, forgot all causes of resentment. In Tenterden's favor, too, he had to admit that, if he were a rival, he was a magnanimous one. For whenever The Pouter called at The Cedars he had a free field. If he had dreadfully few *tête-à-têtes*, it was due simply to the perversity of the adored one. So much impressed, in fact, was our jovial lover by the chivalry of his rival that he often assured Tommy that, if he was to lose the game, it would be a sort of satisfaction to him that the Englishman should be the winner.

"He is a perfectly square man, Tommy!"

"And you are perfectly round, Pop! Ho! ho! ho!"

"H'm!" said the lover, leaning over for a peep at the toes of his boots, "I was speaking metaphorically."

"What's that?"

XXIII.

But this happy winter was gone,—with its bright breakfasts and cosey dinners, its snug readings-aloud during the long evenings, its daily music lesson.

There came—and we have so few of them—there came a perfect spring day. The young Englishman rode to the post-office.

It has come, what he had expected, a roll of music from Schirmer's,—some arrangements for four hands. Bessie had had none. Thanking the postmaster most graciously, and springing upon his horse, he bounded off at a gallop.

But soon the balmy down-pour of delicious warmth overcame both steed and rider, and with slackened rein they crept along at a walk. 'Twas not a day to hurry through.

The soft breath of the south caressed his

hair, played about his moist brow, eddied around him, fraught with the intermingled odors of flowering mead, of upturned soil, of awakening wood,—laden with the love-calls of birds, the hum of insects, the pebbly murmur of brooks released from their bonds. And over the broad, green wheat-fields there danced and quivered a golden haze. And above, there floated, here and there, a speck of fleecy cloud,—all else an abyss of blue.

'Tis the very color of her eyes!

His horse fell a-munching the roadside grass.

A mocking-bird zigzagged past him, beating the balmy air with capricious, disdainful wing, proclaiming, the while, in full-throated frenzy, the cruel perfections of his lady-love; while she, demure Miss, trim in her suit of modest gray, coyly peeping forth from embowered shade, marvels at his antics, and wonders how long she can hold out against the witchery of his brave song.

Faint heart never won fair lady. He tightened the rein.

An unseen turtle-dove tells of his love to all the cool and fragrant wood!

"Shall I alone be silent?" With a quick pull upon the bridle he leaned forward, and soon was cantering up the well-shaded road. Hearing that Bessie was in the orchard, he hurried in that direction, brandishing the roll of music in triumph. But when he came suddenly upon her, he stopped, spellbound.

· Never fairer vision dazzled the eyes of enamoured swain, never pearl had fairer setting. Plunged in a deep revery, she had not heard his approaching footstep. Clad in a dress of summer stuff, flecked with blue upon a white ground, she sat, or, rather, reclined upon a rustic bench, in gracefullest abandon of indolent repose. Above her a peach-tree spread its branches, the vivid, tender green of its budding leaves smothered in dense masses of fragrant blossoms.

In such rosy bower the very goddess of love herself might well have reclined content.

And the fair maid, with sunny head resting against the trunk, saw not the wealth of sheltering bloom, heard not the hum of the innumerable bees, marked not the delicate odors that floated past. Her form lay there in all its loveliness; but her spirit was afar,— revelling in the land of love's young dreams.

And upon her upturned face, the light of heaven, struggling through the incense-breathing petals, sifted down in a rosy mist.

And every now and then, a silly young bee (out, to-day, for the first time, perhaps) darts down and buzzes, for a moment, about the fair dreamer (mistaking cheeks for roses, stray ringlet for nodding jonquil, or vainly imagining the breath of violets), then bustles away on disconcerted wing!

Not Cnidos, nor Paphos, hardly beloved Cythera, ever bore, on beds of amaranth, lovelier burden!

XXIV

THIS very day, while Mr. Edmondson and Tommy were at dinner, their two setters rushed, barking, towards the gate. Tommy hurried out. Spring, which brings back to us the birds and the flowers, had caused to pass along the county road, on their way through the country, a band of Italian musicians, who, liking the look of things, had turned in at the gate. And when Mr. Edmondson, overcome by curiosity, had found his way to the front door, napkin in hand, he saw the party tramping, dusty and footsore, up the gravelled walk, convoyed by Tommy. Our active young friend had his hands full, or, to put it differently, was kicking the soles off his boots, as, black in the face and hoarse with shouting, he scurried round and round the pilgrims; landing a blow, now on Carlo's eager jaw, now on Beppo's resounding ribs. For race-prejudice is not confined to men; and these two handsome brutes, rested from the hunting-season, were for making game of the foreigners,— willing to nip the calf of a fiddler, glad to pin the youngster with the cymbals. It would be something, even to imprint a monogram on the seat of the clarionet's trousers.

The voice of the master ·brought them to a sense of how they were tarnishing Virginia's good name; and they crouched, penitent, at his feet. He, anxious to make amends, begged the minstrels to come up on the porch; but the leader declined, on account of their soiled and travel-stained condition. Clustering under a big sycamore, they were briskly furnished, by a brigade under Tommy's command, with chairs, water fresh from the well, towels, clothes-brushes. After a hearty meal, they were supplied with tobacco, which they peacefully smoked, surrounded by an admiring audience, who, with mouths agape, gazed in wonder upon the strange instruments. The harp was a sort of lion.

"Blessed if dat fiddle ain't got more'n a hundud strings!" whispered one.

"Hukkum you know dat a fiddle? Whar de bow? I ax you dat!"

"Harp? Who dat say 'twas a harp? Marse Jimmy? Oh, he know!"

"Harp?" cried an old woman, in an excited voice; "git out o' de way an' lemme look good! Sure 'nough! Well, I neber did hope to see a harp in dis life. When I got 'ligion and seed de glory of de throne, all de angels was a-settin' roun' a-playin' of jess sich, but I neber did hope to set eyes on de like, here below."

But the violoncello excited a feeling of amazed incredulity. How could mortal man play on such a fiddle,—especially such a little fellow: "Nemmind; you jess wait.

Bound he ain't tote sich a insterment roun'
for nothin'."

Whenever one of the Italians spoke, there
was a universal ducking of heads, with
smothered laughter,—but without discour-
tesy. It was merely childish delight in the
talk as part of the show.

"Buono tobacco, questo !"

"I hear him say 'baccer, jess as plain !"

"An' I hear him say bones. Boun' he got
'em in he pocket !"

Tommy, bold Tommy, ventured, at last,
out of the fringe of audience, and, approaching the harp, looked it over narrowly.

"You play?" asked the harper, smiling.

"Oh, no !" cried Tommy, drawing back,
amid the subdued gurgling of the fringe.

"Oh, yes, come !" And taking the
bashful forefinger of the blushing lad, the
harpist began to pluck the air of "Dixie"
from the strings, amid billowing roars of
delight.

Until we have forgotten how to laugh, life is worth living.

The band began to play.

I shall not attempt to picture the delight, the bliss of the simple auditors, nor the charm of their unaffected ways of exhibiting it. The master sat upon his broad porch, puffing away at his pipe, he, too, enjoying both the music and the scene. Presently the minstrels passed from the martial strains of a march to a more sentimental discourse of sweet sounds. The Pouter's eyes grew dreamy. His pipe went out. The strain ceased.

"Tommy!"

The irrepressible youngster bounded up the steps. His father, passing his arm around his shoulder, began walking up and down.

"Tommy, I have a little scheme. Suppose we keep the band here and give her a serenade to-night—h'm? How does that strike you?

"Serenade Miss Bessie? Splendid! And I say, Pop, won't we get the bulge on Legs?"

It must not be supposed that Tenterden's lower limbs were abnormal. He was a well-made six-footer; that was all. Tommy's nickname was merely a symptom of the aggressive loyalty of the lad. His father's supports were short, and had the air, according to a *mot* of Mrs. Geoff's Judy, of toothpicks sustaining an orange. (But those who heard this speech thought of sour grapes.) To Tommy he was the best of fathers, and without blemish. I am sure the honest fellow would have backed "the governor" in a foot-race, to the extent of his exchequer. In his eyes, to differ from Pop was to lack a perfection.

"You mean Tenterden?" asked "the governor," with sudden gravity. "You don't think, Tommy, that he—h'm?" And he jerked his thumb over his shoulder in the direction of The Cedars.

"After her! Of course he is, Pop! You should see him mooning around! But I say, Pop, I think you have been fooling around long enough, sending me over with partridges and bouquets and things. My advice to you is to pitch in, right away; or Legs will get the bulge on *us!*"

"Pitch in, you say?"

"Why, yes; pop the question, Pop!"

With that they both shouted with laughter; and small wonder.

"I'll do it, Tommy; I'll pop the question —ha, ha, ha!—to-morrow. Not a day later!"

"Good! You'll get the bulge on Legs. Faint heart never won fair lady!" added he, drawing freely on his literary fund.

"Good, my son; excellent!"

"Right after the serenade,—strike while the iron is hot," rejoined the lad, tapping his accumulations of wisdom.

"Good again!" thundered the exultant

parent, bringing down on Tommy's shaggy head an applauding palm.

"Look out, Pop, that hand is heavy!"

"You are in a hurry to see a pretty little mumma installed at the head of the table?"

"And you want to install her, don't you, Pop!"

"Fact, Tommy, fact,—you impudent rascal, —ha, ha, ha!"

"Hold on, Pop; my ear ain't made of leather!"

"I am holding on, ha, ha, ha! But we shall get the bulge on Legs! Ho, ho, ho!"

Vain exultation! Let me wave my seer's wand, and reveal a scene at this very moment enacting in the parlor at The Cedars.

It looks very much as if Legs had gotten the bulge on Pop.

X X V.

MOST of us have been, at times, aroused from a revery by the last stroke of a clock giving out the hour, and still have been able to count, in the chambers of the brain, the impressions which the air has lost. So our fair dreamer, her spirit floating afar, amid the rosy clouds of youthful fancy—though she heeded not, yet did she hear the soft footsteps of her adorer, as he reverently stole away, loath to break the spell that cast about her so divine a halo. Arousing from her dream with a start, she looked about her, bewildered, at first; then caught a glimpse of his receding form. A vivid blush overspread her face, as, with sudden maidenly instinct, she brushed down (though needlessly), about her ankles, the snowy skirts. For a moment her blue eyes were darkened.

It is not without a shock to be looked upon unawares, though only one's soul be in dishabille.

But only for a moment; for she divined, from the roll he carried in his hand, that he had sought her out to show the new music, and, finding her in dreamland, had stolen away through delicacy. And with a sudden rush her heart was brimful of that tender foolishness which has been a buckler to many bosoms in this pitiless, thorn-girt path along which we mortals are inexorably driven, —dimly guessing both the whence and the whither. And she felt, as she rose and slowly sauntered towards the house, wrapped in the warm and scented air of spring, that, if he took it into his head—if he should happen to choose this hour for talking a little " nonsense," she would hardly have the strength to be unkind. He met her at the porch, brandishing the roll in triumph: " And now we can play duos together !"

"How nice!"

"I thought you would like to open the parcel with your own hands." There was a subtle something in his voice,—something new and strange.

"You are very thoughtful," replied she, with a little glance that repaid him, he thought, for all the trouble he had been at in not opening the package.

She sat down on the topmost step of the porch. He took his seat beside her. She tore away the envelope with hands that trembled slightly,—so eager is woman's curiosity. And she smoothed out the fresh, clean music with her dimpled hands, as it lay on her lap, murmuring, "Beautiful! Beautiful!" whispering to herself the successive titles with subdued delight. All save one. Perhaps she did not remark it. At any rate, she passed on to the next.

And as they leaned over the fair pages, their heads were close together. Who can

read notes a mile away? And was he not
'brother Bob's dearest friend?

And a pert little zephyr, seeing them sitting there, so close, so cosey, crept, a-tiptoe,
up, and, plucking away from loosened comb
a fluttering tress of golden foam, fanned it
with ambrosial wing against—blissfullest of
chins—then scampered off, holding both his
sides.

A most ticklish business!

And the jocund elf floats away, borne
on the indolent-eddying, scented breath of
spring. And as he sweeps, on diaphanous,
misty wing, over blooming mead, the flowers,
knowing their master, smiling, nod. And
in orchard and in copse, the nesting birds
twitter shrill welcome.

Nor does he forget, as he passes by, to
breathe upon the peach-bloom damask of
oval cheeks. And maidens gaze far away,
dreaming of coming fates.

Victorious spring is in the air.

XXVI.

"WHICH one shall we begin with?" asked Bessie, dropping down on the piano-stool (as though a trifle tired).

"This," said the young man, placing the music before her, and drawing up a chair (without the least symptom of fatigue).

"That?" asked she, in a low voice, and without glancing at the title. Perhaps she knew what it was. It was the only piece that had a blue cover,—the one, by the way, of which she had omitted to read aloud the title on the steps (where the naughty little zephyr was playing his tricks).

"This," said he,—"That?" said she,—two wretched little pronouns!

Oh, of course she must have known what it was!

It was the Wedding March of Felix Men-
delssohn-Bartholdy.

And as they sat there, he pressing down
the rebellious sheets, and trying to make
them lie smooth, up trips, again, the saucy
zephyr, and, through the open, festooned
window, shakes at them a bloom-laden frond
of twisted honeysuckle; and, with a puff
from his plump cheeks, sends the rich per-
fume circling about their heads.

And two little house-sparrows (just arrived
on a bridal tour from Louisiana),—daintiest,
friendliest of all our birds,—alighting on the
window-sill in pretended quest of crumbs,
peeped in. And the happy little bride said—
or seemed to say—"Chip! chip!" but, just
as likely as not, she meant "There they are!"
and *he* made I know not what reply, but
with knowingest of winks. And away they
darted to the orchard, chip-chipping as they
flew,—but I shall always believe they were
giggling for dear life.

"The darling little things! We frightened them!"

"How happy they looked! Well, are you ready? All right! You come in on the sixth bar, mind. One, two, three, four——"

And there rose from beneath his fingers those opening notes that have stayed the beating, for very joy, of full many a heart,— that have sent a flash of radiance over the faces of many an audience.

Down came Bessie's hands.

"Oh, how stupid!" cried she.

"Once more, then."

Confusion worse confounded. Never was there such blundering! Such a jumble in the bass, too! And he a professor!

Bang, bang, below; tweedledee, above: but no respect for the intentions of the composer,—no beat, no rhythm——

No rhythmic beat! Ah, but what a mad thumping, somewhere! And tender throb makes answer!

"If we could but keep together to the end!" cried she.

"If we *only* could!" sighed he.

Bessie, paling a little, leaned quickly forward. Sometimes notes are a little blurred. They begin anew.

And Mrs. Willis sat in her chamber, wondering that she had not noticed, before, how dreadfully out of tune the piano was.

Never was Mendelssohn so massacred. The little zephyr stopped his ears with his Liliputian thumbs; for he too is a musician,—an Æolian harper,—cunning to evoke, when he will, melodies, tender, vague, bewitching, from whispering reed, from quivering poplar, from sighing pine.

"Oh, where on earth are we!"

"*I* am not on the earth!"

"Tell me where to begin, please?" and she averted her face to hide the flash of an exultant smile. But the smile was not there! Not upon her kindling cheek, not in her brimming eyes! It trembled, rather, deep down in her fluttering heart.

" *There!*" said he, leaning forward and placing an agitated finger upon a line of her part. He thrust forward his arm so swiftly that hers did not have time to get out of the way; and the cheviot and the organdie rustled together.

A most ticklish business!

Lay your hand upon an uncharged electrical machine. It is nothing! But the merest tip of your little finger—if it be tingling!

Boom, boom—fiddle faddle——

" I'll send Reuben for the tuner to-morrow," thought Mrs. Willis.

Bang, bang—tweedledee——

" Oh," sighed Bessie, dropping her hands in despair, " what can possess me to-day ?"

" I know, too well, what possesses me."

Bessie leaned forward quickly, and began studying the notes : " You talk so much, you put me out," scolded she.

"Woman, we are told, is often generous, rarely just."

"Why, I have not uttered twenty words!"

"I know—but——"

"I——"

"Is it really worth learning?"

"It is beautiful—but——"

"But too difficult for me?"

"I wasn't going to say that."

"Well?"

"Well—it is not much—on the piano—but on the organ——"

"On the organ?"

With hands poised above the keys, with wistful eyes devouring her averted face: "Yes, on the organ. But *we* would not be the performers. Some one else would be playing it for us,—for you—and for me—Bessie!"

The blue-flecked organdie rose and fell in thronging beats.

"Let us try just once more," she faltered.

He obeyed with alacrity,—sniffing victory with exultant nostril.

And so the four hands came down once more,—but for the last time. For Bessie made a mistake that put an end to this music lesson.

Every one knows that the various octaves of a piano are as much alike as two peas, even to one who is perfectly calm. But she was not calm. How could she be, with her professor talking and talking and putting her out? At any rate her left hand struck one octave too low. But that brought it square a-top of the professor's right.

"Oh, I *beg* your pardon!" and she covered her face with her hands.

Wise teachers correct errors on the spot. So the good professor instantly took the erring thumb in his right hand, and the ill-advised little finger in his left, and was about to plunge them down upon the correct octave—*there!*—when—he changed his mind.

Was it because the wrist was so limp, the poor little fingers so dreadfully tired? Quick as a flash he strained that hand against his heart, then pressed it to his lips, devouring it with kisses; and against his heart, once more, and again to his lips. And all the while she (for her right hand still covered her eyes) had not the least idea what he was at.

Not so Jenny Wren. She, as she emerged from a crevice in the wall, near the top of the window, saw plainly enough what he was up to. Jenny was an old married woman, and had been watching the world wag a good many summers; still, she was far from having lost her interest in such things: " Look, look, look!" (Tuweetaweetaweetawee) chirruped she to her spouse, who was, himself, peeping with might and main from a walnut hard by: "Oh, we boys are all alike!" rejoined (in the Wrennish) the dapper gallant, with a humoristic flirt of his dandified little tail.

And when the wicked little zephyr (who had crawled up on the sill on all fours) saw that soft little hand resting so snugly; and when he saw, too, a stalwart arm following the line that had been marked out for it— just in the right place—by that belt of blue ribbon, and closing upon it with slow vehemence, he chuckled, he, he! and he chuckled, ha, ha!—rejoicing in the mischief he had wrought. (But *they* thought it was the rustling of the honeysuckle.)

And then another arm went foraging, and brought in a fair head captive, and laid it upon a square shoulder. And for a moment there was blissful rest and peace. But only for a moment; for brief is man's content. And so the sunny head began to duck this way, dodge that,—to left, to right,—now down, now thrown back, with lips compressed in forbidding primness, under which lurked a forgiving smile. And he was so very, very persistent! So at last the weary head fell back upon the hospitable shoulder, and—well?

"Ho! ho!" roared the little imp (but gently as any sucking dove), tumbling backward out of the window in his ecstasy. And falling upon a bed of violets, he rolled over again and again. But the violets barely nodded their heads,—so light was he. And the merry sprite, rising on scented wing of woven hair, went his way, leaving, everywhere, sweet trouble in his wake.

XXVII.

It was midnight. A glorious moon revealed a light, topless wagon at the front door. The master held the reins, faithful Tommy at his side. The tuneful sons of fair Italia were clambering into the vehicle and taking their seats in splint-bottomed chairs provided for the purpose. Around stood a swarm of youngsters handing up to the band, with zealous pride, their several instruments. Even to touch them was honor. A man stood at the head of either horse,— and with reason, to judge by the low, nervous patter of their hoofs on the gravel. Let 'em go! A swift spring forward; a sort of earthquake among the passengers.

"Set hard on dem cheers! Don't, you gwine to git duss on your backs," was the voice of anonymous counsel.

"Don't mind, dem ther'breds spill dem lingo people, yit!" whispered prophecy.

Mr. Edmondson had a fad as regards horses. But two kinds were worth a moment's consideration,—thoroughbreds for gentlemen, mules for the Man and Brother. The thoroughbred was swifter, more enduring, kinder, more intelligent, more courageous, longer-lived,—why, sir——

He was driving a pair of these perfect animals to-night; and hardly fair specimens, for he had taken them in hand but a month before. That did not disturb our friend, however. As a driver he was absolutely fearless.

Notwithstanding that the band had played fully two hours after supper (and had been liberally rewarded by the dusky throng around the sycamore), the wagon had no sooner started down the road than there was a pell-mell rush across the fields, towards The Cedars, of the entire farm force. The

boys led, eager, panting.   Next strode on
the men, while the women brought up the
rear, dragging their children along the path,
one or two even carrying infants in their
arms.   Not a human creature was left on
the farm.

Meantime, the minstrels pursued their
chequered career along their more circuitous
route.   Over the level stretches they flew,—
at one time one colt, at another both, gallop-
ing.   Tommy's Socratic nostrils dilated to
the rushing freshness.   His eyes flashed joy.
The Pouter, his widespread legs stiff as steel
against the dash-board, held the quivering
reins like one who knew how.

But now, the colts, coming suddenly upon
a broad patch of moonlight, swerve violently
to the right.   An overhanging branch swishes
against wagon and passengers, and the colts
dart madly forward.   The Pouter had lost
his hat, but, though his waistcoat shook like
a bowlful of jelly, he sits intrepid in soul.

Never mind, Tommy! We'll get it on our way back.

It *was* no time for collecting hats; for an enormous cow lay in the road, a few yards ahead, peacefully chewing her cud.

No true cow seriously objects to being run over. If you give her time she will slowly creep out of the road. But the Pouter didn't have any time to give her. All the time that there was, the colts were making.

Over her, like deer, bounded the gallant bays. The driver held his seat; but Tommy, as he wheeled a somersault through the air, saw her wild-starting eyes rolling like balls of fire in the moonlight.

Chairs and fiddlers were inextricably intermingled. The cymbalist stood on his head. The harpist lay flat on his back, his heels in the air, while his heavy instrument, coming down on the clarionet's head, laid him low. And when the cow rose, bellowing, with the wagon on her withers, the Italians

15* .

could easily imagine themselves back in Calabria the Seismic.

A most gruesome opening to a moonlit serenade, this basso profondo of a frantic cow!

Tommy, wonderful boy, lit on his feet; and, jumping into the wagon from behind, scrambled back to his place over the commingled minstrels.

The colts reared and plunged, refusing to go forward. The cow looked on in wonder. The Pouter touched the flank of the off colt.

Whizz!

"Look out-a, signor; he kick out-a de brain-a!"

"He can't kick any brains out of you, can he, Pop?"

"Not much!" quoth the sire, exulting in the loyalty of the son.

Down came the whip. Away they went like the wind. But at last they came to a halt in front of The Cedars, the thorough-breds quivering in every nerve.

" Wo-o, boys, wo-o !"

The serenade began.

The annals of music hardly record a shorter.

One note. No more.

XXVIII.

BESSIE alone heard the approaching wagon. Even Tenterden slept the sleep of the just (I am sorry to have to record), while his inamorata lay wide awake, a half-smile parting her lips. Wondering, she arose, crept to the window, and peeped through the Venetian blinds.

But I spoke too fast when I said that Bessie alone was awake. Tiger was not asleep. Tiger (Tige, for short) was Uncle Reuben's 'coon dog. A large brindled cur, good at his trade, and very fierce withal.

"Yes, sir, Tige he part bull; but de reason he so oncommon ambitious, I sprinkle gunpowder on he victuals when he was a puppy."

Whether Tige's ambition was due to this alleged pedigree, or to the stimulating condiment in question, I cannot say; but it led him into a scrape, once, whence he escaped with a modified expression of countenance. Meeting a gentleman, in a narrow path, instead of getting out of the way, he sprang furiously upon him. The hunter addressed a cartridge to Tige's care, and shore clean away his left upper lip, leaving the glittering fangs exposed, and converting him (on that side) into an artificial bull-dog of grisliest mien.

Such was Tige, as he lay beneath the porch, on the night of this peaceful, moonlit serenade.

He, too, we can well imagine, was surprised at the sound of horses' hoofs at that hour. But Tige was, like all dogs, an aristocrat; or, if you will, a snob. He respected people who called on wheels. Giving a sniff or two, therefore, for form's sake, he lay his grim muzzle between his broad paws and awaited events. People who called on people at that time o' night would bear a little watching.

m

Mr. Edmondson had quite set his heart on opening the programme with the softly sentimental piece to which we have alluded; but the leader had made him see that it might be totally wasted if played first: the *bella signorina* might sleep through it all. As the lover had relied much on the emotion to be aroused by that tender melody, he hailed as a revelation the suggestion that they should begin with a rousing strain,— something in the *AWAKE! AROUSE thee, dreamer fair*, line.

As it turned out, the dreamer fair was peeping through the blinds, while the minstrels braced themselves for the thunderous harmonies of their opening chords.

They had been kindly entreated, and would do their very best.

The fiddlers arched their right arms on high.

The clarionet inflated his cheeks till his eyes bulged visibly.

The harper bent him forward, adjusted finger and thumb, fixed his gaze upon the leader.

The cymbals, poised high in the still air, faced each other, ready to rush together.

The flute drew his lips into a pucker that was, even by moonlight, conspicuous for its intensity.

Did a wave of suspicion ripple over Tige's mind? I know not. Nature has denied me the gift of analysis. I confine myself to mere outward facts. He drew in his breath, and shot it out with a force that sent the dust flying. His forepaws moved apart, a trifle, flattening themselves on the ground. His hind feet drew themselves together beneath his haunches, which rose slightly. Rose, too, the bristles along his brindled back. Since his trouble with the huntsman he had had but one lip; that one lip faintly fluttered.

Tommy had turned his back to the horses.

The Pouter straddled his seat, facing the house, the reins lying lightly in his left hand, the light of love and the moon illumining his rubicund visage.

Bessie looked on, wondering.

Tige looked on.

Suddenly there banged upon the stilly night a bang, there tooted a toot, there zimmed a zim, there tweedled the first syllable of a tweedledee.

The first syllable only.

The serenade was over!

For the thoroughbreds made a mad spring. (Wo-o, boys!) Perhaps, had the fates been propitious, they might have stopped with that. But what sound is this!

Imagine a thunderbolt, if you can, hurtling forth from resounding cavern! 'Twas Tige! He did not bark. From a pup, he had never been a dog to waste his voice. But with every bound his back bumped against the floor of the porch.

He did not leap across the road, he did not run, he did not fly. He bounced across, his legs rigid, all four paws coming down in synchronous staccato; and the gravel flew, rattling, before him.

His teeth, on the side where the lip was gone, glittered in the tranquil moonshine. And, fearful to relate, with every bounce he sucked in his breath with raucous, blood-curdling sound.

As though he came not to bite, but utterly to devour.

Monstrum horrendum informe ingens, cui [*labrum*] *ademptum.* An 'twere a buck-jumping maelstrom!

Wo-o, boys!

They woed not, those boys, nor tarried, till, sailing like birds over their owner's front gate, they stood trembling in their stalls, with fragments of their traces dangling about their clear-cut limbs. They had left the wagon and a few chairs (she might sit down, if she would) with our old friend the cow, without asking for a receipt. For she, after the unpleasantness earlier in the night, had decided, with bovine calm, that there was no good reason why she should not, and two good reasons why she should lie down again in the same spot: the dust was soft, just there; and it was notorious that lightning never struck twice in the same place.

And so, rising a second time from her interrupted cud, and standing amid the *débris*, she bent her mild gaze upon the cymbalist (who alone had stayed with the boys so far), and, stretching out her neck, seemed to ask him, with a plaintive low (they had not given her time to bellow), to give a poor cow some explanation of the unusual unusualness of things.

But let us hurry back to The Cedars, where some of our friends are in trouble.

We will find the road punctuated with reminders of the serenade. A chair, a broken fiddle, a disconsolate minstrel, a flute, another minstrel, another chair,—they were scattered all the way from the cow to the scene of their "*AWAKE, AROUSE thee, dreamer fair.*" (And I must here anticipate by acquainting the reader with the fact that the minstrels remained with the amorous widower a week, while their leader was in Richmond, with seventy-five dollars of the Pouter's money in his pocket, buying new instruments and having broken ones repaired.)

But while we have been away, sympathizing with the cow, our gallant Automedon has been having an experience sadly out of joint with the moonlight that lay upon that peaceful lawn.

At the frantic plunge of the colts, on the dread entrance upon the scene of Tige, Tommy tumbled out of the wagon on the farther side, while harp and harper fell next the house. In a trice, down upon the unhappy musician rolled Pop, face downward,—

that is to say, his fingerbowlish waist landed on the "small" of the artist's back.

Science tells us that action and reaction are equal,—that a nose strikes a fist just as hard as a fist hits a nose. The nose, as has been remarked by careful observers, is always of a different opinion. So, had you whispered in the ear of our harpist, as he felt all his breath suddenly bursting through his mouth and nostrils, "Never mind; you are bumping up as hard as he is bumping down," you would have been uttering an eternal verity; but he would have looked upon you as a professional humorist. It all depends upon how you put things. Say to him, rather: True, you seem to have the worse of it, for the moment; you do remind one of a pancake; but meditate on Tige, and be comforted.

There had been a discussion between Pop and Tommy whether the lover should don, on this auspicious occasion, a certain brand-new suit just arrived from Richmond; and on the ground that they would, most likely, be invited in, it had been agreed that the serenade should be illustrated by the new rig. Of this new suit, the coat, when its owner fell, flew over his head.

Now Tige knew and esteemed Mr. Edmondson; but how was he to divine, from the view he had, that there lay before him a respected neighbor? Whoever it was had covered his head, and, as he kicked out frantically, in his efforts to rise, was plucking from the harp what must have seemed to an untravelled dog like Tige, most sinister sounds. And the most knowing of dogs would hardly have been up to surmising that a worthy country gentleman could be there, at that time o' night, enacting the part of lawn-roller to a brother man. The brother man could not be seen, it is true; but his stifled groans and strange, sonorous oaths showed that he was there.

Tige, being no strategist, simply took the chances that offered themselves. He came, he saw, he bit,—bit with all the whole-souled energy of his simple, earnest nature, then, drawing back his full mouth, shook his trophies with a growl of savage triumph. Growled once, shook once, then collapsed,— collapsed in an instant, as though struck by lightning!

It was not that Tommy, blubbering with the noble rage of filial affection, had sprung upon him and broken a club (more accurately, a clarionet) across his embristled back. Tige took no account of boys and their doings. But, with a flash of overpowering humiliation, he recognized, in the very moment of shaking between his glittering teeth that quarter of a yard of cheviot, that he had been rending the garments of a trusted friend.

With hanging head, with drooping tail, with fallen crest, he slunk away to his den.

Meanwhile, there had been scurrying to and fro in the house. Bessie had aroused her mother and Bob; Bob had awakened Tenterden. The two gentlemen descended hastily to admit the serenaders. They lit the lamp.

"What on earth is the row?" said Bob, rubbing his sleepy eyes.

"You see we came over to give you a little serenade. That's one of 'em," said Pop, glancing towards the disconsolate harpist.

"Where are the rest?"

"Damfino!" (gracefully dropping into Italia's soft tongue). "Ask the colts! Ask Tige!"

"It was going to be just a splendid concert," quoth Tommy, ruefully, "but Tige had to go and break it up!"

"By the way, I wonder if the scoundrel—damn a cur, I say—didn't tear my breeches?" observed the lover, feeling under his coat-tails. "GOOD GOD ALMIGHTY!"

" Here's the p-p-piece!" snivelled Tommy.

"Where did you find it?"

"I got it from Tige; the d-d-durned fool was carrying it under the porch!"

XXIX.

"WELL, Tommy, at home again! Now run up-stairs, my son, and jump into bed! Good-night, my boy!"

"Good-night, Pop! All I hate about it is that we did not get any bulge on Legs."

189

XXX.

On the morning after these stirring events, Tenterden had a satisfactory interview with Mrs. Willis; after which he rode into the neighboring village and gave Mr. Warwick, her lawyer and friend, the addresses of some people in the old country who would vouch for his respectability. Meanwhile, it would be proper for him to find quarters in the village, himself. He would ride out every day, so as to continue his lessons in agriculture under Bob, and direct the musical studies of Miss Willis.

In the absence of any society journal to perform that office, Mrs. Geoff's Judy, mounted on Termagant, spent the following week in spreading the news of the rupture between the Willises and the young Englishman, and his consequent hasty migration to

190

the village. These sudden and violent friend-
ships always came to a like end. She had
felt confident how it would be, from the very
first. Well, it would be a lesson to them, at
any rate.

But as the Englishman persisted in riding
down to The Cedars every day, often dining
with the family, often taking tea and returning at a late hour, she had to come out in an
extra, with editorial comments to the effect
that it was nothing more than people might
expect who introduced unknown adventurers
into their families. For her part, she had
known perfectly well how it was going to
end, from the very first. It was not to be
wondered at, of course, that a silly young
girl should throw herself at the head of the
first foreigner that came along; but she *had*
given Mrs. Willis credit for more sense. No-
body could make her believe the monstrous
story that they had set a pack of hounds on
Mr. Edmondson; but if they *had* done so,

they were taking a good deal of unnecessary trouble. Mr. Edmondson was not looking in *that* quarter, *she* knew!

At the end of a fortnight it was remarked that Termagant was growing a trifle thin. But what she had done was nothing. During the following week her flanks were to be covered with foam.

It was Sunday morning. Bessie was absent from church. She was in Richmond, on a fortnight's visit. Tenterden, as was his custom, sat in the Willis's pew. Judy was there. She never failed, rain or shine. She was, in fact, a notably devout young woman, —a not infrequent trait, when one has the sins of all one's friends to repent of. But she found time, .without missing a response, to keep an eye on the adventurer.

Towards the end of the first lesson, a slight movement in the lower part of the church struck on her vigilant ear; and she was about to turn and wither the late arrivals with

stony stare, when she saw the impostor start.
He had a way, as she had frequently observed with contrition, of letting his eyes
wander, from time to time, from his book.
On more than one occasion had she detected
him casting shy glances at Bessie. Actually!
So, now, he had, in his irreverent and idle
way, raised his eyes in the direction of the
new-comers. And when he saw them, he
had visibly started. There was not the least
doubt of it; he started!

It is of the last importance that those who
have the interests of religion at heart should
see what is going on in church; so she
turned and saw that the late arrivals were
Mr. and Mrs. Sanderson.

Sanderson was a young Englishman who
had bought a farm about fifteen miles distant; but he came, occasionally, to Miss
Judy's church (as it was generally known to
the congregation). He had married a girl in
this neighborhood, though Mrs. Geoff's Judy

had steadily refused her consent to the very last. But the young person's parents, finding that he was not only a gentleman in his own country, but took the trouble to continue one in this (a half-rare case), gave him their daughter. They had been married several years, and were provokingly happy; so that Judy was more than ever set against such ill-considered unions. Sanderson was an immense, loose-jointed fellow, and, with his blue eyes, blond beard, and fresh complexion, typically English in appearance; notwithstanding which, his mite of a wife (she weighed hardly one hundred pounds) had managed to convert him into a rabid Virginian. His half-earnest, half-humorous bragging about Virginia (especially her women) made him very popular. One of his sayings was that any country that had invented the julep was fairly entitled to rest on her laurels, without another effort, for a century at the least.

Such was the man whose entrance into Judy's church had made the adventurer start. Sanderson, however, was so busy fanning his little wife, looking up the hymns for her, etc., that he never once glanced towards Tenterden. As they were near the door, they were among the first to pass out of the church; and before Tenterden could overtake the couple, Sanderson had left his wife on the sidewalk and gone to fetch his trap from a side street. Miss Judy was close by when Tenterden, going up behind Sanderson, laid his hand on his shoulder.

"In the name of all that is wonderful, Mainwaring, can this be you?"

"I am under that impression, my dear boy!"

The two men wrung each other's hands.

"You don't know my wife, Mainwaring? Of course not! Come, let me present you to her,—the dearest little girl, by the way, and she will be delighted to know you.

Come!—my dear, this is my old Eton chum, Mainwaring, dropped from the clouds! Since Christmas, you say? Extraordinary, by Jove! Here, jump right in! Where is your luggage? All right! Give us a week. Ah, good boy! Come, Polly, hop in!"

The wee and winsome Polly beamed on the old Eton chum, and seconded her husband's invitation with great warmth.

"I'll be back in a minute. I must run down to the corner for a moment, to see about a little matter."

Mrs. Geoff's Judy happened to be walking in the same direction.

"Your husband seems to have met an old friend!"

"Oh, yes; isn't it nice? Mr. Mainwaring; he has so often spoken to me of him. He is to spend a week with us. But you must know him?"

"Oh, I have met him frequently. He

has been in this neighborhood since before Christmas."

"Is it possible? Yes, so he said. And that Jack should not have known that he was here!"

17*

I⊤ was well that Termagant was tough and tireless, else had the following week's work been more than even she could have endured. People hardly knew Judy, so bright was her eye, so sunny her smile, as she galloped up on the spirited little mare. "Oh, I just can't stay in the house this beautiful weather. And besides, Mrs. Blank, I have *a crow* to pick with you. Why haven't your children been coming to Sunday-school more regularly? Bad weather? Well, it has been horrid, till recently. Never mind, children, we can make up for lost time now. How are your strawberries this season? Oh, no, I could not possibly wait; I must be off. I merely called by, in passing, to give you a *good scolding* about the children. Upon my word, Mrs. Blank, I have not time, and you

ought not to have taken the trouble. However, since they are here I will take one
or two. What nice, rich cream!" (What
makes Mrs. Geoff's Judy so civil, I wonder?)
"They are perfect beauties! Came from Mr.
Edmondson's, you say? Kind neighbor, I
hear. Oh, I assure you, Mr. Blank, it was
no laughing matter. *You unfeeling man!*
They say he was torn to pieces, almost.
Nothing but the seat of his bree—trousers,
you say, Mr. Blank? Didn't set Tige on
him? I am truly glad to hear it! People
are so malicious! Making love to Bessie?
That *is* news, indeed! Well, if that be true,
—mind, I say *if* there be any truth in that
absurd story,—she might go farther and fare
worse. *Very—much—worse.* What, is it
possible? Not heard it? Why it is all over
the county!" (alas, poor Termagant!) "Not
true? It is only too terribly true. Mr.
Sanderson knew him as soon as he laid eyes
on him. Didn't I see the creature start, with

my own eyes? Yes, Tenterden is an *alias.*
Mrs. Sanderson told me his real name with
her own lips. Just to think of poor Bessie's
being entrapped by a wretched adventurer!—
as likely as not a ticket-of-leave man! Hope
for the best? Oh, how sweetly charitable
you two good, good people are! Well, I
must be off. Be sure to have the children
at Sunday-school regularly, hereafter. No
more, thank you. They are delicious." She
smacked her lips. They deserved it; for
they had done double duty.

And she and Termagant were off like the
wind. Life is short, and Judy knew how to
make the most of it. She loved to eat and
to disseminate tidings. She had bitten two
berries with one tooth.

XXXII.

"LET me help you again, Mr. Mainwaring; though Jack maintains our strawberries are not half so fine as those you have in England."

"Not half so *large*, Polly," rejoined Sanderson. "The size of a thing is neither here nor there. Now look at Polly herself. I have seen many girls larger, but——"

"Now, don't make a goose of yourself, Jack!" (Jack had a habit of doing just that, where she was concerned.)

"I don't see how he could help it," said Mainwaring, bowing.

"Ah, you will get on with our Virginia girls, if you know how to make speeches like that!" laughed the pretty little matron. "It sounds as though you had been practising a little too!"

"Eh, old chap? Fallen a victim to Miss Judy's charms?"

Mrs. Sanderson suggested the names of a few other girls in his neighborhood.

"By the way, Mainwaring, speaking of the Willises, you know, of course, the young Englishman who has been spending the winter with them, studying farming?"

"Oh, yes," added Mrs. Sanderson, "Mr. Tenterden. I have been intending to ask you about him. Jack ought to have called, long since."

"Oh, I fight a little shy of my countrymen, at first."

Mainwaring looked from one to the other, smiling, but silent.

A spoon, with a big strawberry, stood still, an inch from the little woman's parted lips.

"Eh?" said Sanderson.

"I—too—spent the winter with the Willises——"

"You! Then of course you know him. Is he a good sort?"

"Not bad—as men go——"

"A kind of chap that a fellow might invite to his house?"

"I believe you would like him——"

"Then I'll call."

"I'm told," said Mrs. Sanderson, "that he is exceedingly handsome. I hear that the girls down there just rave about his eyes and his figure?"

Mainwaring blushed, frowned, and smiled all at once: "I dare say. At the same time, I must add that it is news to me."

"Oh, you men! Why are you so unwilling to hear one another's good looks praised! I am sure he must be just lovely, from what I hear. Describe him to me. How tall is he? Is he as English as Jack? What is the color of his eyes and hair? Is he nice? Is he clever?"

While Polly was pouring forth this volley

of questions, a totally different current of thought was dancing through that shrewd little head,—a prerogative of woman. She saw through the whole business! Mainwaring and Tenterden were both smitten with that lovely Bessie. A clear case of the green-eyed monster! Oh, these men! But how easy they are to see through! Seeing him hesitate: "Well, give me a portrait, so that I may judge for myself."

"Let me see. Well, he is not as tall as Jack, by an inch or so."

"About your height?"

"To a hair-breadth, almost——"

"Well?"

"And I dare say you would say he was not as English-looking as your husband. At any rate, his hair and eyes are dark."

"Very, very dark?"

"Well, I should say about the shade of mine. He wears side-whiskers and a moustache."

"The darling! Jack did in our courting

days, but he is too lazy to shave now. Go on,
please. He wears his beard as you do, then?"

"Precisely. So far as beards go, you
could not tell us apart."

"A very handsome, stalwart figure, I am
told——"

"Well, opinions might differ as to that
about such a figure as mine."

She gave a little smile and bow, as though
to say that, in that event, opinions were not
likely to differ so very widely: "According to
your account, you must be as like as twins!"

"By the way, Polly, there is another re-
semblance,—their names: William Tenterden,
and William Tenterden Mainwaring."

"How extraordinary! In Virginia we
claim relationship on less than that. Any
other coincidences?"

"One or two more: we both strum on the
piano a little."

"Wouldn't it be good fun to see the two
twins playing a duet?"

"And leave Miss Willis out?"

"Oh! If it be a fair question, is there a coincidence there, too? Do you—admire her as much as he does? Though that would be hardly possible from all accounts."

"Hardly, I should say," cried Sanderson, bursting into a laugh. "You know Tommy, of course; everybody knows Tommy, Edmondson's boy. Extraordinary chap, that, eh? I should say so. Well, I met that amazing lad a month or so ago, riding, and he gave me a killing account of this chap Tenterden. He says that he is so awfully gone on Miss Bessie that he feels sorry for him, seeing him mooning around like——"

"Mooning around?" repeated Mainwaring, with a sickly smile.

"Yes, mooning around; and you should have seen the look of woe-begone misery that chap managed to throw into that freckled mug of his."

"It must have been very amusing!" (dryly).

"Amusing! Why, I roared! I was near rolling off my horse. Oh, yes, I remember, —and he said, 'Mr. Sanderson, you ought to see him when he catches sight of her passing around. Why, sir, he comes to as dead a stand as our Beppo at a covey of partridges!' Poor devil, I know how he feels: I was just as bad over Polly,—eh, little one?"

"You were perfectly dreadful, Jack, that's a fact," replied happy Poll.

"Why don't the idiot pull himself together and try his luck, eh, Mainwaring?"

"Yes, why don't he?" echoed Polly. "Every Virginia woman believes, as an article of faith, that when a man loves a girl, she is entitled to hear it."

"He has done so. He has proposed."

"You don't say so!" cried Polly, eager as a war-horse when he hears the blast of a trumpet. "Poor fellow!"

"But he was accepted!"

"Accepted! Oh, I am *so* sorry!"

"Sorry?"

"Of course I am sorry! I don't know this horrid Mr. Tenterden, and Bess and I are such friends, and you and Jack have always been such chums! It is just *too* provoking!"

"You might like Tenterden just as well as you do me."

"Never!" cried the impulsive little body; "I dislike him extremely already. Such a nice little scheme to be broken up by this miserable interloper!"

"But he is just like me——"

"I don't care!"

"Even in name. That is the strangest coincidence of all."

"His name?"

"The name of the lucky dog—would you believe it?—Is William—Tenterden—Mainwaring!"

XXXIII.

"Now sit just here, under this nice old tree, and tell us all about it. You need not make any more signs, Jack; I shan't understand them! Right here shall I sit and hear it all. How you men love mysteries! And what would be the use? You know, sir, I should make you tell me every word; else not one wink of sleep for you this blessed night! There, set it on that little table, Mr. Mainwaring, at your elbow. I gathered the mint with my own hands, and can vouch for its freshness. I think you will find it—h'm?"

"De-li-cious! What do you call this divine mixture?"

"Never had a julep before? By Jove, I envy you, old chap! Making its acquaintance is as sweet as the first kiss of love. Don't pout, Poll; I didn't quite mean it.

Ah, that's a good little girl.   Then you have never heard the story of the Virginia chap who taught the Kentucky chap to put grass in his liquor?   Never?   Good!   You see, there was a chap, once——"

"For goodness' sake, Jack!"

"Well, I'll be good, Poll!" said her big husband, removing her hand from his mouth and patting it.   "But for juleps and the dearest girls on earth I'll back the Old Domin—— All right, Polly; go on, Mainwaring."

No wonder Jack was popular throughout the county!

XXXIV.

MAINWARING was an only child, and was left an orphan, but heir to an estate sufficient to render the study of any profession unnecessary. When he left his university, therefore, possessed of good looks, a robust constitution, and a fortune ample for all reasonable needs, he began the happy life which seemed to lie before him by knocking about the world for two or three years. It so happened that, during these peregrinations, he had met, in Cairo, an elderly Australian, also on his travels, who bore the same name with himself. The old gentleman, who was in poor health, took very kindly to the stalwart, good-humored, and, as he had many opportunities for judging, unselfish and obliging young fellow; so much so that he showed himself solicitous to prove a distant relationship; a whim which the younger man humored through amiability rather than conviction. A few months, however, after his return to England, he was amazed to learn from a law firm of Melbourne, that their client, Mr. Mainwaring, had left him his entire fortune; a windfall by which his income was more than quadrupled——

"I remember hearing of your good fortune at the time," interrupted Sanderson.

"What a lucky man!" exclaimed Polly.

"So I thought at the time, I remember."

"Do you mean to say——"

"I mean to say that that fortune proved an unmitigated curse."

Even while at the university, Mainwaring had taken a lively interest in the condition of the laboring classes and other social questions. But with the moderate, if sufficient, income derived from his grandfather, sympathize as he might, he was practically powerless. He might be liberal with shillings, half-crowns, sovereigns; and he was lavish in that small way; but he felt that he was bailing out the ocean of human misery with a thimble; or even, as he sometimes feared, adding to it. But now this Australian fortune had come to him. And wealth was power. For power he did not care. But it was also responsibility. That, being such as he was, he neither could nor would shake off, he would spend his life assuaging suffering. But how?

Earnest, conscientious, and thoughtful, he set about discovering this how in the most methodical, painstaking way. He read books and pamphlets without number, consulted with reformers and philanthropists, socialists and clergymen. He went from institution to institution planned by others. But the more he observed, examined, thought, the bigger grew his doubts; till, at last, the bark of his enthusiasms and hopes went to pieces on the rocks of scepticism. All efforts to ameliorate the condition of mankind had proved dismal failures—or worse,—and if, here and there, something had been accomplished, the harm done by ill-considered devices more than counterbalanced the good wrought by wiser efforts. He still gave—gave freely—but without hope. For he had become convinced that concentrated wealth, though potent for evil, was impotent for good.

"Behold one illusion gone!"

"But, surely, you could relieve such suffering as came under your eye? And were your friends and relatives all rich?"

Mainwaring lifted his goblet to his lips as if to draw consolation and strength from its fragrant depths; muttering, *sotto voce*, amid the mint and ice:

(If I live a thousand years, and write a thousand books, somewhere, in every one of them—trust me, my friends—you shall find a julep nestling!)·

"*Infandum, regina, jubes renovare dolorem,*" whispered the melancholy millionaire.

" What does that mean, Jack ?"

" It means, Let us wet our whistles and proceed with the harrowing tale !"

" Fib !" laughed Polly, punching his vast shoulder with her ridiculous little fist.

" Go on, Mainwaring. [*Chink !*] I'm with you ; luck !"

" You are quite right to call it a harrowing tale. [*Chink !*] Same to you ! I had flattered myself, before I came into this fortune, that I had rather more friends than most young men. I soon came to doubt whether I had one in the world. Adversity drives away the cowards and sneaks ; but there is the consolation of knowing that the two or three who stand by you are true. But, unfortunately, the good and the true are just the men likely to make themselves scarce when sudden prosperity draws around a man a swarm of parasites and flatterers. So, at least, I found it. A king—and a millionaire —may have friends, but they have no means of knowing who they are. And if there is one thing in the world that makes life worth living, it is friendship——"

" And love ?" suggested Polly.

"Same thing !" put in Sanderson : " love is nothing but red-hot friendship !"

" Perhaps," laughed Mainwaring. " But, to cut a long story short, my ill-omened fortune, as a mere matter of fact, cut me off from all who were my friends, and surrounded me with those who desired to seem such. The former fought shy of me, believing, all the while, too,—ah, that was bitter,—that *I* was despicable enough to avoid *them*. So that I lost not only their regard, but their respect. Nor did I gain that of the horde of snobs and sharks who surrounded me. They despised me, very naturally; not stopping, always, at contempt. In one instance, certainly, I earned bitter hatred.

"Among my distant relatives was a young woman [Polly straightened herself] whom I regarded almost in the light of a sister. [Polly lolled back in her chair]. As she was left penniless at the death of her father, I rescued her from going out as a governess by a yearly allowance. She married a worthless fellow, who, thinking that, as her husband, he would have an easy time, living on my bounty, soon entered upon an extravagant mode of life, looking to me to foot the bills. I did so once, but with a serious warning; which was disregarded. Then came insolence on his part, and from her (when I proved inexorable) a letter full of bitter and insulting reproaches. My cup was full. No; for it was to be fuller. One of my old-time friends, who had met with undeserved reverses, lost his only child through privations which I could have relieved. I had known, in a vague way, that his circumstances were straitened; but he had avoided me. I was piqued. Why does he not come to me? I muttered, in the insolence of wealth. Well, perhaps not, Jack: I hope I was never really that. Perhaps I was hurt that he should think so ill of me; but the result was the same. His child died,—and I could have saved it.

"I could give dozens of other experiences that were discouraging, to say the least; but these two incidents, coming within a week of each other, were too much for me. I resolved to flee from my surroundings. I had seen Europe and the East. I took passage for America. Perhaps there was less. misery there! My departure was, perhaps, hastened by a little incident of a purely personal nature, but I shall not trouble you with that. When I reached New York——"

"Stop, old boy; you don't know Polly. If you don't tell her that incident of a purely personal nature, she won't sleep a wink to-night, Curiosity? Ugh!"

"Oh, it is a very dull story——"

"Perhaps we might be of a different opinion," urged Polly.

"I can see, from the way her eyes are dancing, that she feels sure there is something in it about—eh, old chap?"

"Oh, I *love* Love!" cried little Polly, clasping her hands in fervid entreaty.

"I'm afraid you will have to give in, old boy. Luck!" (*Chink!*)

The old boy gave in. (*Chink!*)

It would seem that our hero (Polly was glad, on Bessie's account, that the affair had been so prosaic) after dodging, for a few seasons, sundry enterprising mammas, had put an end to such persecution by proposing to the daughter of a widowed neighbor. They had been friends from childhood, and seemed likely to be nothing more. But one evening in June (now nearly a year since), under the triple influence of music, moonlight, and roses, he had suddenly proposed, and been haltingly accepted.

The period of their engagement had not proved a happy one to Mainwaring. He was constantly chilled by the inexpugnable reserve of his betrothed. "Have I not promised to marry you? What more proof do you want?" Her mother assured him that it was merely her daughter's undemonstrative way; but this did not satisfy Mainwaring, who knew how impulsive, frank, and affectionate she had been from childhood.

The end came one evening about a week before the day set for the marriage. She acknowledged, in bitter tears, that she did not love him: she had merely hoped that she would learn to do so. She respected—yes, in a certain way loved him too well to carry the deception to the bitter end. She did not say that she had felt it to be her duty to love him. That, he read between the lines. She had heroically resolved to sell herself for the sake of her young brothers and sisters; but her native nobility had triumphed at the last moment.

"And now, Mrs. Sanderson, you see the three blessings that followed in the train of my good luck. First, I lost faith in my ability to be of any use in the world; secondly, it drove away from me my true friends, and brought about me, in their stead, a horde of sycophants; thirdly and lastly, it was very near enabling me to buy a wife who loved another man. In my desperation I fled to this country. But—what does Horace say, Jack?"

"Don't know I'm sure: forgotten all about the old duffer."

"Well,

> 'Patriæ quis exul
> Se quoque fugit?'"

"What does that mean, Jack?"

Jack, pressing his brow in his left hand, and with his goblet in his right, bowed his head in thought.

"Oh, yes:

> "An exile from his native land
> Oft finds a duck on a foreign strand."

"I don't believe one word of it! Is he telling me the truth, Mr. Mainwaring?"

"His rendering is sustained by the facts of the case."

"Oh, I see! Poor silly old Jack!"

"She is the dearest little girl, Mainwaring; luck!" (*Chink!*)

"Well, wishing to bury myself, for a while, I chose an hotel where I was least likely to meet any of our compatriots. My dropping a part of my name was an accident due to the vivacious intelligence of the hotel clerk. I was writing my name on the register, and had gotten as far as "William Tenterden," when it suddenly occurred to me to ask whether I could have a room. "Certainly, Mr. Tenterden. Let me see,—yes, No. 93, Mr. Tenterden.—Here, show Mr. Tenterden to No. 93. London? Ah!" I was amused at the briskness of the young man. He had christened me anew. Very well, I would be Mr. Tenterden. I liked the fun of the thing. Besides, I should be more effectually hidden under that name than if I bore my own.

"I spent a month poking about in all sorts of places in New York, and was not long in discovering that there was about as much hopeless misery there as in London. Meanwhile, in all this great metropolis, I knew not a soul. I had fled from the world, but I had not escaped from myself. For weeks I endured the agony of despair, till—at last—would you believe it?—I seriously thought of——"

"Oh, Mr. Mainwaring!"

"Yes. You hardly realize, perhaps, how true it is that extremes meet here, as elsewhere. There is the despair of the man destitute of everything; but there is another despair, and as bitter, of one for whom all things have been provided. He, like the other, lacks hope. The most miserable mortals that I have known have been young men (what I say applies to them only) like myself, who, from their very abundance, could imagine no good thing that the future could hold in store for their sated bodies and jaded souls. Perhaps your attention has never been called to the subject, and you would doubtless be surprised to learn how frequent suicide is with this class. Look here." (Taking from a pocket-book a number of newspaper slips.) " Here is a list of victims that I collected at a period when I took an almost morbid interest in such subjects. Let me read you my latest clipping:

"'SUICIDE OF AN AUSTRIAN MILLIONAIRE.

"'VIENNA DESPATCH TO THE LONDON CHRONICLE.

" 'The suicide of Herr Stephen von Kegel, a well-known millionaire and man of fashion, and one of the handsomest men in the empire, has created an immense sensation in Vienna. Herr Kegel was not only already very wealthy, but was heir to a fortune of about twenty million florins. He was quite a young man, and was one of the most prominent sportsmen in Hungary. The cause of his suicide is absolutely unknown. On Thursday he was at Pesth, and he was, it was declared, in the gayest of moods, and yesterday he shot himself on his father's estate near Stuhlweissenburg.'

"The cause of his suicide was absolutely unknown! Was not the hopelessness of an utterly useless life cause enough? No wonder he was in the gayest of moods, when he had once made up his mind to——"

"Oh, Mr. Mainwaring, don't talk in that dreadful way!"

"Oh, it is all ancient history with me now. I find farming a most soul-satisfying occupation, and then—you see——"

p

"Oh, I see, old chap! Shake? Congratulations, I'm sure—luck!" (*Chink!*)

"By the way, Mrs. Sanderson, there is a small matter which has been worrying me not a little. You see, I have asked Bessie to become Mrs.——"

"Oh, I am sorry for you, young man! Just think of it! Bessie has undoubtedly written *Mrs. William Tenterden* and *Bessie Willis Tenterden*, hundreds of times, just to see how it looks. And then to be told—oh!"

"You have put your foot in it, old boy," laughed Sanderson.

"My dear madam, please devise some way of getting me out of the scrape!"

"That's right, old chap; leave it all to the dear girl. By the way, Poll,—just one more, eh? Awfully auspicious occasion, you know! Ah, good little girl!"

XXXV.

It was Saturday morning, a week later. There was a knock on Mr. Warwick's office door. "Come in!"

Mrs. Willis entered, pale and agitated: "Oh, my dear old friend," cried she, seizing his hand, "what *shall* I do!" and, dropping into a chair, she burst into tears.

"My dear madam, what can be the matter?"

"My poor daughter! Tenterden is not his real name! I heard it only last night, and I did not sleep a wink. Judy Geoffrey says——"

"The she-devil! I beg your pardon, madam; but that woman! So she has discovered, has she, that his name is Mainwaring? What would you say if I told you that I have known it for months?"

"Oh, Mr. Warwick, and not tell me! And there was poor Bessie——"

227

She brushed the tears from her eyes and looked up. Mrs. Willis was amazed. This old and tried friend was smiling,—yes, actually laughing! What could it mean!

"My dear madam, dry your tears and listen to me. You will smile, too, before I get through with my story. However," added he, drawing from a pigeon-hole a package tied with a red string, "first read these three letters. They reached me this morning, and I was going to deliver them to you this evening."

Mrs. Willis ran her eye over the contents of the letters with feverish haste, breaking into ejaculations from time to time.

"Very satisfactory; but how is this, Mr. Warwick? They all say he is a man of wealth?"

"So I see," replied the lawyer, his fingers interlaced, and twirling his thumbs. His eyes were shut, his lips parted with a happy smile.

"Why, he often told me that he intended

to try to lay by a little money, from time to time, so as to be able to purchase a farm after a while!"

"Oh, yes, I have heard him tell you that, myself; I could hardly keep my face straight."

"And you knew all the time!"

"Certainly."

"For heaven's sake, Mr. Warwick, explain the meaning of all this!"

"With pleasure. I am at liberty to do so now, for I had a little talk with him on his way to Sanderson's.

"Exactly why he changed his name, I do not know,—a mere whim, I suspect. But as his pecuniary dealings through me were important, he had to tell me his real name. It was a professional secret, however; for, as he justly observed, it would have been annoying to you to know that he—a member of your household—and not some imaginary English investor—ho! ho!—had taken up the mortgage on your farm."

Mrs. Willis gave a quick little satisfied nod.

"In taking up the mortgage, his original object was to aid Bob, in a judicious way. But, after a while, another motive came into play,—yes, very obvious. He made no confidant of me in that matter; a lawyer's ear hardly seems a fit depository for such—ah—ah—in fact—well! But from his cautioning me several times to keep his pecuniary circumstances a profound secret, I began to suspect that he had conceived the romantic idea of winning Bessie's heart, unaided by the glamour of fortune." (A little hitch in Mrs. Willis's breath.) "When he gave me his English references he acknowledged that this had been his motive; but he still—— There they go now!" cried the lawyer, making a dash at the window, upon which he rapped vigorously; then, hastening to the door: "Where are you going?"

"We are going to spend the day with

Mrs. Willis," answered the chirpy voice of Mrs. Sanderson.

"She is here in my óffice."

While the gentlemen were looking for a boy to hold the horses, little Polly rushed into the office and embraced Mrs. Willis with fervor: "Isn't it splendid! He and Jack such old chums,—and then Bess and I! Oh, I am just too happy!" And the little woman fairly danced.

"Mrs. Willis," said Sanderson, entering the room, "this is my old friend Mainwaring. we were neighbors in the old country, as boys, and chums at college. And you have had him in your house all winter and never gave me a chance at him!"

Half an hour later the party set out for The Cedars; the gentlemen leading, Polly holding the reins for Mrs. Willis,—a risky arrangement. And she was near smashing things a dozen times, so busy was that little tongue of hers, picturing the future that was to be so happy for everybody : "And to think of Bessie being the mistress of that fine old place across the creek! And oh, he has already written for architects and landscape-gardeners to come on! And she is not to know a word about all these fine doings till after the wedding! Jack and I are to run down to Richmond, and I—oh, what fun!—am to break the news as to the change of name. And his gifts to the bride—we have consulted about all that for hours. He has decided upon—oh, I forgot! Well, I suppose I ought to tell you. Well * * * and * * * and * * *, isn't that just too splendid? Dear Bess, won't she be just too fine! Oh, I'm just crazy : that's all!"

XXXVI.

A FEW days later Sanderson and his wife were in Richmond. They had just sent up their names and were awaiting Bessie.

" How on earth are you going to begin, Poll ?"

" I'm sure I don't know. Ah, here she comes !"

Polly handed Bessie a thick letter from her mother: " Read it; Jack and I will entertain one another."

But Bessie would not; so she and Polly fell to, while Sanderson twisted about, uneasily, in his chair. Presently Polly drew to her a sheet of paper which lay on a table at her elbow, and, dipping a pen into the ink, began to scribble away with much ado; without, however, uttering one word the less.

"What on earth are you doing, Polly?"

"I always did dote on scribbling."

Every now and then she held out the paper at arm's length and studied it, dropping her head first on one side and then on the other, to get a better view. At last, after a grand flourish, she laid down the pen, and raising the paper, contemplated it with great satisfaction.

"Ever since I gave my hand to Jack, it has been growing more English, don't you think so, Jack?" And she thrust the paper under his nose. Jack took it and glanced down the page: "By Jove!"

"Let me see it," laughed Bessie.

"Give it to her, Jack."

At the first glance Bessie gave a pretty little blush. (Oh, Polly, how dreadfully silly you are!) Polly had written half a dozen times, in various hands, large and small, round and pointed, the words *Mrs. William Tenterden.* Then followed, in as varied

chirography, *Mrs. William Tenterden Main-*
waring. Bessie looked up with a puzzled
expression, then read aloud the following:
Faithfully yours, Bessie Willis Mainwaring.
"What do you mean by all this, Polly?"

"Mean? What do people ever mean by
scribbling? When I was a school-girl, I delighted in writing names in that way, imagining myself the bride of various heroes of
romance with ever so lovely names. I wrote
myself down Mrs. Arthur this, Mrs. Reginald
that; but I never once thought of putting
myself down as Mrs. John Talbot Sanderson; yet I came to that in the end. Mainwaring is lovely, I think,—Bessie Willis
Mainwaring! Umgh!"

"Don't you think Tenterden has a nice
sound?" (A little blush.)

"W-ell, yes,—nice enough; but just hear
the two, one after the other: *Mrs. William
Tenterden*—so so!—Mrs. WILLIAM TENTER-
DEN MAINWARING! *That's* a mouthful for

you! If *that* was to be your name, now! Don't you agree with me, Jack?"

"I always agree with you," replied Jack, ready to explode. His little wife's vivacious dexterity of mind, so typically American, was a constant source of amused amazement to the big Englishman.

"What is the matter with you two to-day? Am I to wait till some beautiful prince of a Mainwaring presents himself? Why, pray, didn't you think of that earlier, and induce your husband's old friend to pay you a visit? Who knows what might have come of it! But let's see what mother has to say. Why, how astonishing! She writes that all the trouble Mr. Warwick was at in writing to England was useless,—that, if we had only known that Mr. Sanderson and Mr. Tenterden were old friends, Mr. S. could have told us all about him! What *can* she mean?"

Sanderson cast an appealing glance at his wife.

"Well, you see, Bess, Mr. Mainwaring, when he arrived in this country,—oh, yes, he is in this country,—took it into his head to be known by his mother's name; so he dropped the Mainwaring, and called himself Tenterden; so, of course, Jack didn't——"

"Called himself Tenterden!"

"Certainly; so you are to be Bessie Mainwaring, after all!"

Bessie started, ominously catching her breath. Crafty Poll threw her arms around the trembling girl:

"Isn't it just too GLORIOUSLY ROMANTIC!"

That word won the day.

"Poll," said Sanderson, as they walked back to their hotel, "in the immortal language of Tommy Edmondson, you are a honey-cooler!"

.

XXXVII

It required infinite tact, keeping Bessie in
the dark as to the gilded future that awaited
her. Bob and his mother were often at their
wits' end. As for Polly, she being fifteen
miles away, was out of the scrape, till a few
days before the wedding, when she and Sanderson drove up to The Cedars, so as to be
in the thick of the fray. I am afraid Polly
fibbed dreadfully, upon occasion. There was
a bevy of bridemaids, from a distance, in the
house. Whenever Polly found herself alone
with one of these, the poor little woman was
like to burst with her tremendous secret. It
was agony to her; for silence was not one of
Polly's points. As it was, her meaning nods,
her lips tightly compressed in obtrusive self-
control, filled the young girls with burning
curiosity. At last, at one in the morning of

the great day, when three or four of them were clustered in one room, talking themselves hoarse, instead of being in bed, asleep, Polly, with her hair hanging down her back, and dressed in a loose wrapper, thrust her head in at the door: " Be off to bed, this instant, you silly creatures. But, oh, girls, if I could only tell you! Spul-lendid! Good-night! Pleasant dreams,—and be sure to look your loveliest to-morrow morning." There was a pell-mell rush to seize her, but she was gone; and the slam of her door was the knell of their hopes. But Polly felt better.

Two arrangements in regard to the wedding were unusual. Mainwaring had particularly requested, and Bessie had consented, that the honeymoon should be passed at The Cedars,—" I have been *so* happy here," he urged; further, the wedding-feast should be at Bloomingmead. That her betrothed had bought this fine old (if somewhat dilapidated) place, and that her home was to be just across the creek from her mother and Bob,— so much she had been told; and it made her very happy. True, she feared the purchase had been a severe strain on his resources; but he had bought it to please her!

Mainwaring had wished, by this wedding-feast, to make a handsome response to all the hospitable attentions he had received in the county; but he could not ask Mrs. Willis to give the entertainment, while he footed the bills. It was Polly who was inspired to suggest that Mr. and Mrs. Mainwaring should, immediately after the ceremony, receive all their friends at Bloomingmead. It was to be a grand affair, and Polly set to work organizing her staff. I am sure the reader will be pleased to learn that of this staff Mr. Edmondson was the chief. "What? Bear malice? I hope I am not that kind of a man! Have I not trotted her on my knee, many a time, when she was a baby? No,

indeed! Mainwaring may say what he will
about his English mutton, but if the saddle I
am going to send from that five-year-old
Southdown wether don't—well!" And no one
could have been a more indefatigable aide-
de-camp than our admirable young friend,
master Tommy. He and his pony scoured
the country, engaging scrubbers to put the
old house in order, to polish the wide barn
floor,—borrowing people's cooks and cooking
utensils, crockery, knives and forks—everything that was needed.

And, during all this time, Termagant stood
in her stall, stamping and fretting, and switch-
ing her tail at the flies that persecuted her.

'Twas a dull season for the society journal.

XXXVIII.

THE happy day has come. The ceremony is ended. All eyes are bent in admiration upon the fair young bride, as she walks down the aisle, then along the paved walk to the street. There is a halt. The carriage is not there. . . . A dozen young volunteer runners dart up the street: "Here dey is, Unk Reuben! Dey done married, an' at de gate a-waitin' for you!"

Then were to be heard the proud hoof-beats of high-steppers; and Uncle Reuben, holding the reins, emerged from around the corner, where he had lain in ambush. Two noble bays, bravely accoutred, their silken coats glistening in the sun, dashed into the street and up to the gate, while behind them rolled silently an open carriage, new, elegant, perfect in all its appointments.

242

But Uncle Reuben! Ah, it was a joy to behold the old man. He was adorned in a suit that Bessie's grandfather had once worn. It had lain in his chist thirty years,—blue broadcloth, buff waistcoat, resplendent gilt buttons. Upon his honest breast bloomed a prodigious bouquet; while long streamers of white ribbon floated out behind his prehistoric hat of wondrous form.

Great was his costume; but greater than his costume was Uncle Reuben. 'Twould have broken his heart had he known that coachmen, in Mainwaring's country, were expected to sit stiff as frozen statues. He could not have done it. The memory of old days came over him; and, as he moved off with his precious freight, his chest bulged, his elbows stuck out, his shoulders, forgetful of rheumatis', played like those of a defiant boxer. And, swelling with pride, he rocked to and fro like a tall ship upon the hoary sea. This team, this carriage was something like!

Oh, no, he had no idea of exhibiting their speed! Let the people have a chance to look. "Dey hadn't seen de like sence b'fo' de war! Let 'em look good. Wo-o-o, boys!"

And the impatient horses, held down by a firm rein, with tossing heads and quivering nostrils, danced down the village street as though they walked on eggs. "Jess look at Unk Reuben! Ain't he jess a-settin' back, who but he!"

Yes, take a long look at him, and a lingering. Those proud horses are not his, nor that costly carriage,—and he is old and poor. Yet he rejoices. So let us, too, rejoice that in these days of *væ victis* and the devil take the hindmost, such splendid fragments of loyalty are left us—for a season.

Reaching the end of the straggling village, the old man gave his team their way, and our couple were soon far in advance of the foremost of their pursuing guests. Presently the road left the open and plunged into a shady wood. It was then that, for the first time, Bessie, feeling that they were alone, looked about her.

"What carriage, what horses are these?" said she, with sudden wonder.

"They are yours," said Mainwaring, taking her hand, and (just as likely as not) squeezing it.

"Mine! Oh, *Will*, what dreadful extravagance!" And, laying her hand upon his arm, she looked up, with knit brows, into his tender-smiling eyes.

Any man who shall blame Mainwaring has never been sweetly scolded by a beautiful bride with whom he is driving through a cool, shady wood, with the enemy half a mile in the rear. There sat Uncle Reuben, it is true. But then, coachmen should always sit like frozen statues. And was an active young man, accustomed to out-door sports, to sit with his arms in his lap forever? So——.

As for poor Uncle Reuben, he couldn't

help it. For some months he had been keeping his eyes open, and been putting two and
two together, with the shrewdness of his
race. "Talk po', does he? Umgh-humgh!
Oh, yes, I hear him. Umgh-humgh, c'yarnt
fool Reuben. Been here too long, chile."
So, as he heard no reply to the charge of
extravagance, he thought he must steal a
look at the groom's face. Besides, the
wheels had just run over a root; had it
jarred Little Mistiss?

"Oh, Lordy, I ax your pardon, young
mahster. I was afeard dat root mought 'a'
shake you up. Nemmind, Little Mistiss, I
won't look round no mo': 'fo' Gaud, I won't.
What's ole Reuben, any way? He ain't
nothin'. He ain't got no eyes, no ears, no
mouf, no nothin'. Besides, ain't you done
married out un a book an' all? You ain't
nothin' but chillun, any way; so go on wid
your confectionments; Reuben ain't gwine
tu'n he hade no mo'."

Of all the coachmen that he had ever seen, Mainwaring thought this one the most charming.

"All right, Uncle Reuben; but mind,— those horses need watching." And he slipped a note into the horny hand of the old man.

"What I tell you, Kesiah? Talk po', did he? Who he fool, I wonder."

XXXIX

I SHALL not attempt to describe the reception,—a combination of picnic, barbecue, and ball. Everybody wandered where he would, feasted when hungry, made himself at home. Edmondson, as generalissimo of the revels, came out exceeding strong: "Go off and enjoy yourselves," said he to the bride and groom; "I'll keep things moving." And, in point of fact, they, freed from all responsibility, did wander off to a secluded dell, and there, seated on a moss-grown log, talked love for one solid, delicious hour.

There was a real city band, which, at four o'clock, took position in the barn, where the Pouter opened the ball with an enchanting imported widow, and—rejoice with me, reader —met his fate.

"Now, that's what I call business," remarked Tommy to a comrade. "Pop has been throwing away his time chasing these young pullets. Now he is crowing round what I call a hen. But she is a stepper, ain't she? But, Lord, look at Pop! Don't he shake a lively toe? Round-dances? No, not for Pop,—arms too short. Get her? You bet!"

And he did,—and did well. Mrs. Geoff's Judy didn't give her consent, and thinks still that it was all a mistake, somehow; especially since she had heard that Mrs. Edmondson has said that she didn't blame Bessie, but she couldn't see what that dried-up old thing could have been thinking about when she let such a chance slip. And as for Tommy, his mamma can't understand why people thought he was going to be such a nuisance. A nicer boy she never saw. His nose was fast growing into shape, his freckles were disappearing; in fact, he was certainly going to turn out a really handsome man.

I am sure I never said anything to the contrary; and, in bidding Pop and Tommy good-by, it is with feelings of hearty respect and warm good will.

As we catch a last glimpse of Mrs. Geoff's Judy, she, too, is happy. For she has secured the landscape-gardener as cavalier, and, seated with him in a cool corner, is sipping champagne and nibbling *pâté de foie gras.*

The architect, a handsome young fellow from New York, created, at first, quite a furor among the neighborhood girls, with his picturesque, artist-face and beautiful, dark eyes; till it leaked out, unhappily, that he had a lovely wife of his own, at home; after which he had to lean upon the saddle of mutton for support, and steady his nerves with a julep. So even he was happy.

So were they, all of them. And, to all of them, good-by!

X L.

THE bridemaids, with Jack and Polly, were taking tea with the happy pair at The Cedars. With one exception, everything had gone beautifully. There was one thing that made the bridemaids wretched. The groom's gifts to the bride had been, unhappily, delayed on the road. (Polly, who was in the plot, knew better. They had been locked up in Mr. Warwick's safe for a week.)

There was a knock at the front door. Reuben went out and returned.

" Mr. Warwick man done come wid some things."

Polly flew out of the room, and, a moment after, thrust her head in at the dining-room door: " Ev-er-y-*body* come into the parlor !"

A wild flutter of skirts. Mainwaring rose, lit a cigar, and sat down again.

But the scene in the parlor! Parcel after parcel was handed to Bessie, who untied them with eager fingers; and, as she lifted the tissue-paper, lovely heads were bumped together, over the exquisite and costly products of Tiffany's art. There were long-drawn breaths, and oh-oh-ohs without number.

Bessie was untying the last package. She suddenly laid it upon the table. "I don't understand all this," said she, with a bewildered, anxious look.

"I will tell you all about it," said Polly, putting her arms around her. * * * * * * "And, Jack, tell her about the ancestral silver, over in England!"

"No end of it," quoth Jack.

"And, oh, Bess, he is going to take you over, next month! And you can see it with your own eyes!"

"Oh-oh-oh, *Bess!*" ohed all the bridemaids with conviction.

Wide-eyed, like a startled fawn, the young

bride stood for a moment. And upon the azure there was a sudden glitter, as of dew upon violets. And she ran out of the room, leaving a startled silence behind her.

The bridemaids stood, with parted lips, breathless, half-smiling—

As though, even through that closed door, they hoped to catch the murmur of a most pleasing sound.

"Somebody kiss me quick!" said Jack.

"Pooh!" poohed Polly, she, too, taking aim at the door with her off ear.

22

BESSIE stopped suddenly, close behind the deceiver. He heard the dear rustling; and, leaning back, smiled at her, over his shoulder. And she, springing forward, clasped his new-reaped chin in both her hands; pressed his head convulsively against her snowy neck. Then (what could he do, with his helpless head twined about so closely by those smooth, round, tender, shining arms?)— then:

"You aw (!) ful (!) fib (!)ber (!)"

"I shall (! !) never (! !) tell (! !) the truth (! !) again (! ! ! !)"

And so, a bad beginning made a good ending.

254

FINIS.

ᒐ